My eyes travel to the large casement windows that overlook the lake. The sky over the lake is an oppressive gray—twilight mingled with the threat of rain. The water, reflecting the sky, is leaden, and the wind from the north sends foaming whitecaps crashing against the shore.

I try to think calmly about the ghost. How can I? Every time I recall the things I've seen, I end up shuddering, my mind skittering away from logical analysis. I drift into a fitful sleep and have an odd dream; I am apprehensively walking in the gray evening through the mist swirling over the shores of Lantern Lake. A figure is coming toward me. Even before he reaches me I know who he is.

Then Reid is beside me, his warm fingers wrapping over mine.

Dear Reader:

Thank you for your continuing support of First Loves and your many helpful suggestions. Just as you have requested, we are now including mystery and suspense elements in our books. We are also publishing more stories with the same characters, and have added a new romantic suspense series by Becky Stuart, the Kellogg and Carey Stories. Look for *Journey's End,* the first of these, in October.

And check out our new covers. We have listened to you! From now on you will see that our heroes and heroines will look just like the characters in our books, and more like you and your friends.

Nancy Jackson
Senior Editor
FIRST LOVE FROM SILHOUETTE

FREE SPIRIT
Katrina West

First Love from Silhouette

Published by Silhouette Books New York

America's Publisher of Contemporary Romance

SILHOUETTE BOOKS
300 E. 42nd St., New York, N.Y. 10017

Copyright © 1985 by Katrina West

Distributed by Pocket Books

ISBN: 0-373-06158-7

First Silhouette Books printing October 1985

10 9 8 7 6 5 4 3 2 1

America's Publisher of Contemporary Romance

Printed in the U.S.A.

RL 7.0, IL Age 11 and up

First Loves by Katrina West

Meadow Wind #148
Free Spirit #158

KATRINA WEST lives in Detroit with her husband and two children. Her work has appeared in *The Detroit News* and the *Detroit Free Press*. She holds a B.A. and an M.A. in English from Wayne State University, where she also spent two years teaching as a graduate assistant while working towards her master's.

Chapter One

It's funny how you can change your mind about someone, and how quickly it can happen.

Last spring, for instance, when Mom told me she'd be marrying Zack Morris and that we'd be moving into Strand House to live, I took it the way any other normal fifteen-year-old would: I was ecstatic.

About the marriage part anyway.

Zack Morris and my mother. I couldn't believe it.

Zack, after all, is *the* top-rated DJ in these parts. He's on WHWL evenings, Monday through Friday, and *everyone* at Lakeview High listens to him. He's funny and loose and just a little bit crazy. Hardly the kind of guy I would have thought the Widow Benton—as Mom used to jokingly refer to herself—would decide to marry.

Not that Mom isn't a doll. She's pretty and sweet and a hard worker. It's just that she's one of the most down-to-earth and practical people I know. She works as a reporter for the *Lakeview Herald*—which is how she met Zack, doing a profile on him for the paper—and when you see her in her conservative wool suits, with her long blond hair pulled to the back of her head in a neat knot, and her forehead creased in thought as she poises a felt-tip pen over her notepad, you'd never in a million years imagine she'd be attracted to a guy who regularly makes the scene in flannel shirts, suede vests, jeans, and cowboy boots.

I was surprised all right. Nice surprised. In the beginning anyway.

Maybe it's true, what they say about your never really knowing a person until you've lived with them. I've lived in Strand House with Mom and Zack for close to three months now, and I've gone from thinking Zack Morris was the best thing since peanut butter to avoiding him like the plague.

Mom keeps telling me that I'll love him once I get to know him better.

I'm waiting.

In the meantime, not too surprisingly, I've found that having Zack in the family has complicated my life.

Last Wednesday, the first day of school, I walked into the building and it was as though everybody had turned into some sort of hotshot reporter—and I was the latest newsflash. For a while I didn't mind the attention. Although now, three days later, it's getting kind of boring—I mean, it's Zack who's the top-rated DJ, not me. But I guess when you've got a celebrity in the family it does funny things to people.

Last year, for example, Dina Farrell—who's a cheerleader and who can be pretty aloof most of the time—would have just passed me by in the hallway with maybe a brief nod. But today she is barreling down on me with a smile that is dazzling in its verve, and I know, even before she arrives at my locker, what she is going to ask.

I know because ever since last spring when WHWL-radio held their Dine-with-the-DJs promo and she managed to win a meal with Zack she has been one of his biggest fans.

Dina stops in front of my locker, her blunt-cut, sleek black hair swinging forward with the sudden pause in motion.

"Kara, you look great," she gushes. "Now tell me—is it true? About your Mom and Zack, I mean. I missed the first couple of days of school—the family got back late from our trip to the Smokies—but Elise Howard just told me Zack Morris is your new stepfather. I mean, is it true?"

I look at Dina patiently.

"Yeah, it's true," I say, giving her my best so-what's-the-big-deal look. It doesn't work. Dina, who is supposed to be very cool, lets out a shriek as shrill as if the Lakeview High Rockets were scoring a tie-breaking touchdown in the fourth quarter of a championship game.

"But Kara, you didn't say a word last year. You didn't let anyone know."

"It all happened pretty fast," I say, twirling the combination on my lock and avoiding her eyes. It's pretty obvious that Dina is one of Zack's true believers and that it clearly wouldn't pay to let her know I am less than crazy about him. It's also pretty obvious, from Dina's next few words, that she's no good at reading minds.

"Oh, it's just too much, Kara. It must be the neatest thing—having Zack Morris for a stepfather."

At that moment the bell rings and, sliding my books out of the locker, I make my escape from Dina, who tries to get me (big surprise) to promise I'll sit with her at lunch.

I mumble a noncommittal "I'll see," and hurry off to make it to world history. I don't have any intention of breaking Oreos with Dina.

I have always eaten lunch in the Press Room with the gang from the *Eagle*. Lunch is when a lot of our best ideas for the paper get discussed. And besides that, the idea of eating lunch with the crowd that would be at Dina's table didn't appeal to me.

Only certain kids make it into Dina's group. It's not like the other cliques at school. Most of them are casual and more a result of common interests than anything else. But Dina's crowd isn't like that. They're extremely statusy. I mean most of the kids drive around in the latest model Mustangs and 'Vettes and are into designer jeans, designer shirts, and designer everything. I honestly believe if there were designer sandwich bags and designer combination locks Dina's crowd would be using them.

Last year I never could have kept up with them. Not with Mom as the sole supporter of my sister Beth and me. Mom's salary from her job as a reporter for the *Lakeview Herald* only stretched so far, and with Beth in college we had to be careful. That's why I guess it still seems a little odd to me to be living in the new house with Mom and Zack, and to have things so different financially.

After living in our little apartment, Strand House is a little like living in a museum. It's a big rambling home built on a hill overlooking Lantern Lake. It was constructed in the 1920's by a local bootlegger, Jack Strand, who, as the stories go, disappeared a few short years later under mysterious circumstances.

Zack bought the place three years ago. Despite its prime location—the littoral of Lantern Lake is studded sparingly with houses that only begin to sell at six figures—Strand House had, Mom said, stood vacant for years and gotten quite run-down. Zack has had it beautifully restored and now, once again, it's the stately mansion that it was in its prime.

It's the sort of place that I'm sure Dina and her crowd would find impressive, but, since the day we moved into it, I've hated it.

Mom tried to convince me it was just a matter of scale. She said when you've spent most of your life in a small apartment and then find yourself in a place with fourteen rooms, most of them oversized, it's only natural that there will be a period of adjustment.

All I know is that there is something odd about Strand House. Things happen there.

Outside the window in Mr. Berrien's world history class, three or four scalloped brown leaves detach themselves from the branch of a tall silver maple and dance down the sunlight to rest on the cool, green lawn. I sink into my seat and repress a sigh.

Then I spot him.

As if I didn't have enough troubles.

Day three of school and Reid Tyler still doesn't know I'm alive, celebrity stepfather or not.

Reid is new this year at Lakeview. He's seated a few desks ahead of me, one row over, so I have a pretty good view of the back and side of his head. The way I feel about Reid, I'm sure that if they gave trophies for the backs and sides of heads, he would have one on his mantel.

How could he miss? Even from this odd angle he is every inch a winner: dark, beautifully trimmed hair, a strong corded neck set on muscular shoulders, and a firm square jaw.

Sometimes when I answer a question in class he turns around, and then I see thick, almost straight, black eyebrows, a high, wide forehead, a nose that is slightly aquiline in profile, and eyes like chips of blue sky.

Mr. Berrien makes his entrance. Tall and slim he has graying hair and a reputation for giving a lot of quickie quizzes. He drapes his tweed jacket over his chair and launches into an exposé of political chaos in the city-states of ancient Greece. Mr. Berrien goes on and on, and I'm glad he has decided to lecture today rather than to carry on a question-and-answer routine. With Reid so close I can't really concentrate on the politics of Greek city-states and, more than that, I don't want Reid to turn around and look at me the way he does sometimes when I answer one of Mr. Berrien's questions.

Mostly, I know, because I'm afraid he'll have the same reaction to the New Me that he has always had—indifference.

I can't help but think that if I were Beth it would be different. When my sister was doing her stint at Lakeview she never had any trouble getting any guy's attention. Of course, Beth had a few things going for her, the way anyone who looks like a California surf queen and has the personality to match would.

With Beth and me it's a clear-cut case of apples and oranges. All of my life people have been comparing the two of us, and the remarks have usually filtered down to comments like: "Beth, you are absolutely stunning, a beauty, real *Vogue* material, no question. And, Kara, you are so—" (pause, and then with lots of enthusiasm) "—*cute*."

Don't you love that word? *Cute*?

Yeah, teddy bears are cute too, but I don't know too many people who want to look like one.

Cute. Well, I guess it covered the extra-thick specs that until last Saturday were Me. My optometrist Dr. Braden says that I have the worst case of myopia he's seen in a fifteen-year-old in the last three years. And I guess if you look at it from a certain point of view, a flaky one in my book, then you might have considered the specs "cute." I didn't. When Dr. Braden informed me last month that the myopia had definitely leveled out and that he was fitting me for contacts, I almost let out a whoop and kissed him.

Mom tells me I look great with the new lenses. She keeps talking about the "beautiful new me." She claims I've "blossomed" over the summer, that I've lost my baby fat.

Okay, so I did lose ten pounds over the summer. But it was purely accidental. I guess in a roundabout way I have to give Zack the credit for the svelte new me. I spent so much time this summer avoiding him that I skipped quite a few meals at home and spent more time plowing through the calm clear water of Lantern Lake than I would have normally.

Mom sees it differently.

Personally I think she has read one too many makeover articles in her *Glamour*s and *Redbook*s because last Saturday, the same day I got my contacts, she insisted that I drop into Scissors and have Vicki, Beth's favorite stylist, whip up a new hairdo for me. Obviously Mom was hoping to underscore the thorough transformation. I humored her.

I thought maybe Vicki was going to do something quite original and christen it the "Kara Benton" or something. Instead she just asked me about my lifestyle; I told her about school, my job two days a week at the Sunshine Day Care Center, and that my preferred form of exercise during the coming fall and winter would be ice skating.

I told Vicki that all I wanted was hair that didn't fly into my eyes when I did spins and jumps and backward bends on the ice—that was why I was wearing my shoulder-length hair pulled back and clipped at the neck with a barrette.

Vicki took a long, thoughtful look at my locks and started snipping away. She gave me a Dorothy Hamill. So much for originality.

Actually, though, it doesn't look too bad. To tell the truth, I really like it. Vicki says it suits the shape of my face and I've found that it's easy to take care of—wash and wear, which is perfect for me. With my job at the center plus all the time I put in at the rink I don't have a lot of free time to spend with a comb and brush in front of a mirror.

Mom thinks the new hairdo looks great. And even Zack took a moment to tell me I look nice.

I think Mom sees this as a big production number—you know, like those old Hollywood movies on the late show where this dowdy girl with no fashion sense takes off her horn rims and pulls the pins out of the knob of hair on top of her head, and suddenly she's this stunning beauty in flowing chiffon doing a spin and twirl while twelve violins play in the background.

Sure.

I don't know if Mom realizes this, but I'm not exactly the chiffon-swirling type. Although just today, just this particular Friday morning as Mr. Berrien drones on and on, and Reid continues to ignore my existence, I wish it were all as easy as the old flicks make it out to be.

Outside a cloud passes and a bolt of sunshine, midmorning angular, streams over me in the classroom like a spotlight. *Presenting*...Kara Benton...New and Improved! Tada! And then, closing my eyes for a moment, the way I used to when I was a little girl making a wish, I do it; I visualize myself walking up to Reid with a big smile on my face, greeting him, and starting a conversation.

I open my eyes and look down at my jeans. The sun picks out a speck of white lint on my right knee. I tweeze it off with my fingers. There, now I *am* perfect, I tell myself. And perfect people don't have any trouble talking to guys like Reid Tyler.

Then the sun disappears abruptly behind a cloud and, perfect or not, I feel a little depressed.

It seems like half-past-never before Mr. Berrien winds up his comments by discussing the legacy of the Greek polis. Finally the bell rings and I am able to gather up my notebooks and march purposefully down the aisle. My heart is beating traitorously fast. When I get to the point in space where out of the corner of my eye I can see Reid standing at his desk, I notice sleek black hair and a cheerleader uniform. A quick glance confirms Dina's presence—she is planted in front of him, smiling up in his face like a model for a toothpaste ad.

Swallowing hard I continue walking and—I can't deny it—a part of me is terribly relieved.

Coward, I accuse myself, and I can feel my cheeks burning.

"You okay?"

I look up quickly, almost guiltily. Carl Markham is standing just outside 103 as I exit the classroom. I have known Carl since kindergarten—we both went to Walt Whitman Elementary together. It seems that I can't visit the library after school without finding him seated at one of the carrels, bent over a textbook. Like me, he is on the staff of the *Eagle*.

"Sure, I'm okay, Carl. Why do you ask?"

"You just looked a little funny is all," he says. "Kind of preoccupied or something. But since you're all right, mind if I walk you to algebra?"

"Hmm?" I say. My attention once again is riveted on Reid, whom I can still see, together with Dina, winding his way down the long first-floor corridor.

"I'm headed to 112, Kara," Carl says. "Algebra. I think you're going that way, aren't you?"

"Uh-huh," I answer absently. My eyes track Reid until he and Dina disappear at a turn in the corridor.

Carl is saying something. I struggle to listen.

"You're looking good, Kara," he says. "I like what you've done with your hair."

"Thanks," I say with a shortness that is almost rude. I am remembering Dina moving down the hallway with Reid. I am only half-listening as Carl speaks.

"So how about it?" Carl asks.

"What?" I ask.

Carl fixes his eyes on me with a penetrating expression.

"Before I repeat myself for the third time," he says, "let me clue you in on something: I don't think Reid Tyler is your type."

My cheeks go red.

"And who says I have any interest in Reid Tyler?" I demand.

Carl looks down at me with a half-smile quirking one side of his mouth.

"Just this feeling I've got," he says. "Call it a reporter's instincts. Call it ESP. Listen, Kara, he's not your type."

A hot spark of anger flashes inside me. Carl has a lot of nerve, I think, telling me what to do.

"And can you tell me exactly why he's not my type?"

"It's obvious, isn't it? He's part of Dina's crowd. Those guys are a bunch of airheads in dress denim, and you know it."

"How do you know he's part of her crowd, Carl? It's only the first week of school."

"Oh, c'mon, Kara, you were at the lake this summer. You saw him with Brad and Larry and the rest of Dina's gang."

That, of course, was true. Her crowd hadn't used the lake too often, but the few times they'd appeared I'd seen Reid with them. They had kept to their own stretch of beach all through the summer. Even over vacation Dina's crowd avoided mingling with the other kids from Lakeview.

"You don't need a guy like that in your life, Kara," Carl is saying.

"Look, Carl," I answer. "I didn't ask for your advice. For your information, I can take care of myself. Okay?"

"Hey, what's with the touchiness? That's not your style."

Angrily I scan Carl's face for any trace of sarcasm, but all I can see in his warm, brown eyes is puzzlement.

He's right, of course. I have always been pretty easygoing. But his remarks touched a raw nerve.

Except it isn't exactly the way he puts it. What upsets me most of all is not the fact that Reid isn't my type. I'm absolutely certain that he *is* my type. What bothers me is that *I* am obviously not Reid's type—and the way things are, it seems there's absolutely nothing I can do about it.

Chapter Two

E*e-ee-ee-ee-ee-ee-ee-ee-ee-ee-ee-ee-ee*.

Noon. Lakeview's first-floor bell, conveniently situated one short yard above my locker, shrills our imminent half-hour of freedom. Impatiently I chuck my books into my locker and yank out my brown bag.

Tavy, who is waiting for me, notices my disgruntled mood.

"What's the story, Kara?" she asks, hugging her journalism folder to her chest. I look up and notice the WHWL bumper sticker pasted at a diagonal on the back of the folder—which does nothing to improve my black mood. Not you too, Tavy, I moan inwardly.

DAR-R-R-LIN! the sticker reads under the station's Gothic-print call letters. "DAR-R-R-lin!" is one of Zack's trademarks—it's how he addresses his listeners when he signs off each night.

"It's what Carl said, Tav."

I had filled Tavy in on my exchange with Carl as we had walked to our lockers from chem class.

Tavy and I have been best friends since freshman year when we shared homeroom and discovered our mutual passions for J.R.R. Tolkien, old Beatles tunes, and chocolate-covered peanuts. Tavy is a future drama major. She has already starred in two productions at Lakeview. She certainly has the looks to make it in the theater, I think—perfect oval face, large expressive brown eyes, and pale blond hair, which she is wearing, today, French braided in back to just below her shoulders.

"I hate to think about it, Tavy, but maybe Carl's right."

"About Reid?"

The lunch bell stops its banshee wail and I nod. "I mean every time I saw him at the lake last summer he was always with Dina's crowd."

"You mean the Living Dead in designer jeans?" Tavy comments. "Look, don't worry about it. The school year is young. Who knows? He may turn out not to be a fashion zombie after all. And who says Carl is the last authority on who's right for you anyway?"

I shrug. "It's sort of a moot point, Tavy, isn't it? I mean, here it is, three days into the school year and he still doesn't even know I'm alive."

"No sparks, huh?"

"Sparks? Are you kidding? Not even static."

Tavy shakes her head and sighs dramatically.

"Men," she murmurs, doing a perfect imitation of Marlene Dietrich's husky German accent.

I chuckle despite myself.

"C'mon," she says. "Race ya to the Press Room."

We break into quick loping gaits and in less than thirty seconds we've navigated the winding stairwells that lead to the second floor where the journalism room is located.

The neatly lettered sign over the inside archway to Room 215 reads THE PRESS ROOM. Rich Winters, a fellow reporter, made it in woodworking shop out of a scrap of pine and hung it outside the journalism room. The Press Room is where a lot of the kids who work on the *Eagle* eat lunch. Nobody knows how the tradition started, but Mrs. Ferris, our journalism teacher, is pretty loose about rules. Her attitude is, if it helps us produce a better paper, it's fine with her.

Usually I love our get-togethers in the Press Room, but today, for some reason, I'm not feeling all that up about it. Probably it's because I'm remembering Dina and Reid heading toward the school cafeteria together. For the briefest of moments I had longed to take Dina up on the invitation she'd extended this morning, and had visualized myself sitting down with her crowd. But I quickly shook off the impulse.

I just didn't like the way Dina's bunch operated, and the lunchroom was no exception. Somehow they have made it understood that the two tables at the south end of the cafeteria are theirs exclusively. Those two tables might as well have brass plaques marked RESERVED bolted down onto their orange Formica faces. Nobody at Lakeview would dream of sitting there if they weren't part of Dina's crowd. Some kids had tried it last year—and gotten a taste of life in the Arctic. As the interlopers put it: You were lucky if they asked you to pass the pepper.

Looking around 215 I can't help but think how different the *Eagle* crowd is from Dina's bunch. Spread out around the room in a variety of relaxed poses, we manage to make 215 look like an illustration for the casual-living section of a magazine.

Carl is perched on the marble windowsill, his legs dangling over the edge, the sun shining highlights over his neatly clipped light brown hair. Gary Leach and Ben Carlin, who do sports and straight news for the paper, are at the back of the room sprawling over the table where we do our paste-ups and galley proofing.

Tavy, a carton of strawberry yogurt in her hands, is resting her long lean legs over the arm of a chair adjacent to the one she is sitting in. Keith Dresler, our editor, is sitting on Mrs. Ferris's desk, munching on an apple. As of this summer Tavy and Keith, who is a senior, are unofficially going steady, which means they don't seriously date anyone else.

Keith is medium tall with broad shoulders and an intense air. He talks a lot about nuclear disarmament, urban blight, and poverty in the Third World. Despite his skill with the written word, he has definite plans to enter medical school and eventually run a free clinic in the inner city. Tavy, who just as definitely plans on making a splash on Broadway someday, has no idea how they will ever be able to mesh careers.

Tavy is not quite as idealistic as Keith, or as good a student, but she's full of more enthusiasm and fun than anyone else I know. Nobody exactly understands the chemistry between them, but there is something about their mismatched levels of intensity that works.

I toss my shoulder bag down onto an empty desk and then hoist myself upon the windowsill next to Carl, my brown bag dangling from one hand. Just as I'm withdrawing a plastic-wrapped peanut-butter-and-jelly, Tavy finishes spooning her yogurt and looks up brightly from her empty carton.

"I've got this terrific idea for a feature," she says.

Eyes are raised from sandwiches and milk cartons, and rest on Tavy.

"A pizza war," Tavy says.

We stare at her blankly.

"A pizza war," she repeats. "We could run it as part of our consumer series from last year. Remember? The kids loved it. We did sneakers and video games and fast-food eateries. What we'll do now is rate the pizzas they serve in all the eateries around Lakeview High. Get the low-down—who serves what around here, the best, the worst—the real truth."

Eyebrows rise in consideration.

"How many pizza places are there around Lakeview anyway?" Keith asks.

"If you're talking a five-mile radius," Tavy says, "there're five: Pizza Corner, Pizza Palace, Luigi's, Pizza House, and KC's."

"I thought KC's was an arcade," Keith says.

"It is," Tavy says. "But they have terrific pizza. Pretty good burgers, too."

"So how come we've never been there?" Keith asks, raising an eyebrow over the carton of milk he's drinking.

"Poor atmosphere," Tavy says, shooting me a quick smile. I know she is remembering the time last August when we stopped at KC's for Cokes and burgers, and discovered that the arcade had become the latest official hangout for Dina's crowd.

While I think about that incident I remember that that was the first time I saw Reid. I later learned from Tavy, who somehow always manages to find out everything about everybody, that his family owned one of the homes on the lake.

"So how about it, Kara?"

"Hmm?" I stir from my reverie to note Tavy's exasperated expression.

"Wake up, kiddo," she says. "How about it—you and me and Keith and Carl doing the pizza article?"

"I don't know, Tav," I say. "It's the time factor. I mean, with my job at the center."

"You mean you're still working at the center?" Carl says, his voice tinged with surprise.

"As a matter of fact, yes," I say. "Is there something wrong with that?"

"Uh, no. Of course not," Carl says, flustered. "It's just that you'd think with Zack as your stepfather—" He stops, embarrassed, but I know what he means.

I'm not ticked at Carl. It's funny but everybody expects that with Zack as my stepfather I'll quit my job at the center. I won't though.

First of all, since I plan to study pediatric medicine someday, I think it makes a lot of sense for me to learn firsthand what kids are all about. Secondly, the job is one more way to keep my distance from Zack. By the time I get home from the center he's usually left for the studio. And, lastly, the simple fact is I enjoy working with the kids, which is the excuse I tell Carl.

"Look, I know you're pretty busy, Kara," Tavy is saying, "but if we're methodical, we can hit all five places over the next couple of weeks, and then I can write up the article for the first issue of the *Eagle*. It'll only mean about an hour at each place."

"You're being very persuasive," I say.

"Well, think about it, Kara," Tavy continues to coax, "a little camaraderie from your pals plus all the pizza you can eat."

"When you put it that way, how can I refuse?"

"Great," she says, her brown eyes sparkling.

"So when do we start?" Carl asks.

"If nobody has any objections, why don't we start tonight?" Keith suggests. "How about pizza at Luigi's around seven?"

"Is that okay with you, Kara?" Tavy asks.

"I work this afternoon," I answer.

"We'll pick you up from the center."

"Tav," I sigh. "Will you ever let me give you no for an answer?"

Tavy looks at me, eyes wide with a show of mock hurt that is quickly chased away by a chuckle.

"Sure," she says. "All you have to do, Kara, is produce a letter from your personal physician attesting to the fact that you're fading away fast and association with a future star of stage, screen, and television is hazardous to your health."

"You mean my word won't do?"

"Nope."

"I'll see you tonight."

"At seven."

"Right."

Since Tavy and I no longer live in adjacent apartment buildings, as we did until Mom and I moved into Zack's home, I find myself bicycling home from school alone. It's about three miles from Lakeview High to Strand House by way of Orchard Trail, an old two-lane road lined with towering elms and poplars.

There aren't many houses on Orchard Trail. Unlike our old apartment, which was located in a highly developed area of Lakeview, Strand House is set in what I regard as a relative wilderness. It is surrounded by two whole acres of woodlands. A PRIVATE PROPERTY sign at the foot of the gravel road that curves up the hill to the mansion warns off intruders. As I swing my ten-speed up onto the gentle slope of the hill's base, I wonder why I feel as though the sign is meant for me.

The wind rustles through the woodlands, and the slanting rays of the midafternoon sun bleach birch trunks a brilliant white and pick out hints of autumn yellows and golds. The air is as crisp and fresh as harvest apples.

I should, I think, be exhilarated. A normal girl would be, wouldn't she? A normal girl would probably be thrilled to live in Strand House and have Zack as a stepfather, wouldn't she? Then why was I being so difficult? Why had I let things deteriorate the way they had between Zack and me? Couldn't I have found some way to hold on to the good feelings we had had about each other only last June?

Strand House looms over me, a red brick Georgian-style box shrouded by elms and cypresses, veiled in ivy, like a secret in the woods. Aside from the garage, the only other building for two or three miles around is the housekeeper's cottage, a whitewashed clapboard structure that stands about thirty yards distant from the mansion, also on the crest of the hill.

Zack rarely ever opens the cottage. We have a part-time housekeeper, Mrs. Curran, who is not a live-in, so the cottage is just used for storage.

I lean my bike against the thick trunk of a nearby cedar. As I straighten up one of its low-lying branches brushes against my cheek like a cool caress.

In the opening between the eastern wall of Strand House and the row of elms flanking it in a formal line, I can see down to Lantern Lake, the pale blue water stippled with silver.

It was there on that lake that they had found Jack Strand's boat, empty and abandoned. The story went that he'd gone out on the lake one clear and balmy evening, and simply disappeared.

Some people theorized that he'd either been drowned accidentally...or by gangster associates. But no body was ever found.

Ever since then, those Lakeviewers who tend to be hardheaded realists point to the fact that, excluding the house itself, Strand had liquidated most of his considerable assets, which had then disappeared with him. They conclude that he had simply cut loose, one step ahead of the law or his gangster friends, and staged his disappearance on the lake.

The more romantic residents, on the other hand, hold that he actually died on the lake, probably at the hands of those same friends. They offer a wide range of grisly explanations for the nonappearance of his body—ranging from burial in an abandoned well to burial in a pair of cement overshoes.

There are even Lakeviewers who will tell you they've seen his ghost peering out of the windows of the housekeeper's cottage or walking along the shore of Lantern Lake; a tall pale figure, glistening wet.

"Kara." A soft voice murmurs my name, and a hand closes over my shoulder. I am about to shriek when I whirl around and spot long blond hair and a T-shirt with a university logo.

"Beth!"

"What on earth is the matter? You look as though you'd seen a ghost."

I take a deep breath and then laugh with relief.

"Sorry, Beth. I was looking out over the lake and thinking about Jack Strand, and I guess I let my imagination carry me away."

Beth laughed. "Do I look like a ghost?"

"Are you kidding? You look great," I say. "As usual."

Beth stands back. She is giving me a look of cool appraisal from head to toe, and a small smile plays over her lips. For a moment Beth is silent and I'm sure she's going to give me a you-call-this-progress look. Instead she just nods.

"Uh-huh," she said. "You definitely are looking good."

I am waiting for the other shoe to drop. "Oh, c'mon, Beth."

"What do you mean, 'Oh, c'mon, Beth'? You definitely look terrific."

I shrug.

"Sometimes, Kara," Beth says, exasperated, "I'd like to just shake you. You look—"

"Terrific," I break in. Sure, I think. I look so terrific that guys like Reid find me totally irresistible. "Look, Beth," I say, "let's change the subject. When did you get here?"

"This morning. One of my friends at the U decided to drive to Detroit to surprise her parents with a visit, and I hitched a ride."

"You mean you managed to tear yourself away from your studies?" I asked wryly. In addition to everything else, Beth is the family's star student.

"Well, the summer semester's been over for a week now. I would have come by sooner, but I had a couple of late papers to work on."

"Is Zack here?"

"No. Mom said he had a meeting with the studio brass—they're kicking around a few ideas for a Halloween special. Something like that. Gosh, Kara, he sounds like quite a character. You wouldn't think someone like that would be Mom's type. I mean, I always think of Mom as down-to-earth and businesslike. Zack sounds like a real cutup. I mean, I've heard some of his shows up at the U—the kids love him. He's so funny and loose and—"

I fix Beth with my best ironic stare.

"What's the matter? Did I say something wrong?"

I shake my head no. For an impulsive moment I am on the verge of spilling my guts to Beth, telling her exactly how I feel about Zack and Strand House. But I don't. What would be the point?

"At least you've had a chance to see the house," I say.

"Is this where they had the reception?"

I nod. "In the drawing room. It was pretty small—just Mom's friends and some bigwigs from the station."

"I'm sorry I missed the wedding," Beth says.

"Mom understood. She was happy for you—getting that scholarship for the summer study program."

"Good old Mom—always the practical one."

"Yeah, always the practical one," I echo. "Just the sort of person you'd expect to go marry a crazy DJ."

Chapter Three

We pull open the thick oak doors to Strand House, and a cool gust of breeze blows in from the lake behind us. The massive crystal chandelier that hangs in the foyer tinkles gently as though stroked by invisible fingers.

"This house is just *beautiful*," Beth murmurs, taking in the formal rooms that open off from either side of the foyer. "You must love living here, Kara."

"It's different."

"*Different?* Is that all you can say about it?"

"Well," I hedge, "I'm not a history buff like you, Beth. I just don't get all stirred up about rosewood end tables and rose brocade upholstery. I mean to me this is all sort of—of—creepy.''

Beth laughs. ''You don't know what creepy really is. You ought to try living in a flat built over a garage with three other girls. Our rooms look as though they've been done by a decorator bent on revenge.''

''I don't know,'' I say. ''Maybe Mom's right. Maybe it's just my imagination, Beth, but things have hap—'' I stop myself, remembering again there's no point in getting Beth all worked up when it had probably just been my imagination working overtime—those odd occurrences. ''Anyway,'' I say quickly, ''I don't mind *my* room—maybe because with all my furniture from the apartment it's the only room that seems like a part of the twentieth century.''

''Kara, this house was only built in the '20's.''

''Maybe so, but it's an exact duplicate of an eighteenth-century structure. Apparently Jack Strand was a history buff, too. If you ask me the architect was just a bit too successful in his efforts. This place feels ancient to me.''

I shrug. ''C'mon,'' I say, starting up the thickly carpeted stairway. ''Let's go up to my room. I have to bicycle down to the center in a few minutes but you can fill me in on your plans for the weekend while I put my school gear away.''

"Well, they're not that exciting," Beth says. "Tonight I'll be getting together with a few of the old gang around five. Maybe tomorrow I'll finally get to meet Zack."

I repress a sigh. Good luck, Beth, I think to myself.

It's a ten-minute bike ride to the Sunshine Day Care Center, and it is almost four when I push my front tire into the rack that fronts the building. The center is housed in an L-shaped tan brick structure and accommodates sixty or so children who range in age from two-and-a-half years to six.

Large and airy and spotless, the rooms at the center feature child-sized furniture and low, open wooden shelves stocked with plenty of books, games, and puzzles.

I lope into the center of the room I work in and find Jill Fuller peeling oranges to serve as a snack. Jill is new at the center this fall and supervises the group I work with.

"Kara!"

Before I can even say hello to Jill I find myself tackled by an excited, breathless five-year-old. My assailant is Nikki Marsh, a tiny girl with a headful of bright red curls, who seems to have adopted me as an instant big sister since she made her first appearance at the nursery school last Wednesday.

I bend down to give her a hug, and her wide blue eyes brim with pleasure. She is a bubbly little girl whom Jill describes as "energy seeking an outlet."

"I made a collage today," Nikki announces proudly. "With tissue paper and Elmer's glue," she adds. "I'll show you."

"That's great, Nikki. I'd love to see it," I say, smiling at her eagerness.

"Hi, Kara," Jill says, approaching me as she wipes orange juice from her fingers with a paper towel. "Nikki's brother will be picking her up today."

"My mom can't come for me," Nikki breaks in. "She's going to an air robots class after work."

"A *what*?" I ask, laughing.

"She's started an air robots class," she repeats. "To get exercise."

"Oh, you mean she's taking an exercise class," I say to her. "Aerobics."

"That's what I said," Nikki insists, slightly offended. "Air robots."

I laugh again and stoop down to give her a little hug before she runs off, dashing toward the easel where paints, brushes, and paper are waiting to be transformed into a masterpiece.

The afternoon passes quickly into the evening. Parents arrive and collect their children at odd intervals, and suddenly it's six-thirty.

Jill is playing picture lotto with one small cluster of children, and I am sitting cross-legged on the pale blue carpet, reading *Green Eggs and Ham* to another small group. Nikki, one of my bunch, suddenly jumps up.

"Reeeeeeid!" she exclaims, running toward the door.

I glance up and find the doorway framing someone familiar. It's Reid Tyler. He's swooping Nikki up into his arms and twirling her around as she giggles in obvious delight.

"Reid," Nikki says as she lights on solid ground once more, "this is Kara. She's nice."

I should feel embarrassed, but Nikki says it so energetically and so matter-of-factly that her enthusiasm momentarily blots out my self-consciousness.

"Hi," I say, glancing up at him over the Dr. Seuss book.

"Hi," he says. Is it my imagination or does his face look a little strained? "I didn't know you worked here."

"That makes us even then. I had no idea you were Nikki's brother."

"That's understandable," he says. "Especially since we don't look anything alike and we both have different surnames. Actually," he explains, "Nikki is my stepmom's daughter from her first marriage. My mom and dad got divorced two years ago and my dad remarried last year.''

As he speaks Nikki skips the short distance from the coatrack to Reid's side, her cheeks dimpling as she purposefully deadfalls against him. It's an affectionate collapse.

"Whoa, take it easy, Nikki," Reid says, and turns to me again.

"Uh, don't you write for the school paper?" Reid asks.

I nod. "Right. Feature articles mostly."

"Uh-huh, I thought I saw you in the journalism room around lunchtime."

"Right. A lot of us use the Press Room then to work on the paper."

"Yeah? Then I guess we'll be seeing each other more often in the future."

"What do you mean?"

"Well, if that's one of the places where the staff of the *Eagle* meets, I'll be there."

"Oh, I didn't know you were taking journalism. You're not in my afternoon class."

"I'm in the morning session."

"So you write?"

"Hey," Reid says, with an easy grin, "do I write? I intend to be one of the crack investigative reporters in the country in a few short years."

Smiling, he is even more handsome than when his face is in repose. My heart does a flip-flop.

But if there are any sparks coming from his direction I'd need a magnifying glass to pick up on them.

"Ready to go, Nikki?" Reid asks.

She nods.

"Bye," I say, watching the two of them leave. It's only later, when I find myself almost serving the guinea pig's pellets to the goldfish that I realize how dazed this brief encounter has left me.

"I didn't know that you knew Reid Taylor," Jill says, as I recover and start to put a puzzle tray back on one of the shelves. She's sitting a few feet away from me, rocking a sleepy three-year-old in her arms.

"Huh? Oh, yeah. He's in my world history class."

"He's quite an attractive guy," Jill says.

Does she think I'm blind?

"Yeah," I say.

"Am I getting the wrong impression or is there something about him you don't like?"

"*What?*"

"Well, it's just that you were awfully cool to him just now."

"Me cool?" That's a new one.

"Well, if you want an unsolicited opinion, yes. That's the way I saw it."

"Well, what about *him*?" I demand. "I didn't exactly see warmth oozing from every pore of his body."

"Well," Jill says, "sometimes it's hard for a guy to show he's attracted to a pretty girl without some encouragement."

I must look as startled as I feel because Jill's next words indicate that she's correctly interpreting my reaction. "Well, for heaven's sake, Kara, you know you're pretty, don't you? I'm sure I'm not the first person to tell you that?"

"Oh, c'mon, Jill."

A smile plays over Jill's lips and she shakes her head in a disbelieving manner.

After the last of the children is picked up, Jill and I finish our clean-up in record time. I don my yellow poplin jacket, grab my purse, and emerge from the relative warmth of the building into the brisk coolness of a misty autumn twilight.

Reid's unexpected appearance and Jill's words have unsettled me in an odd way. I am deep in thought as I pump my ten-speed up Longdale Avenue, and it's not until the familiar green van pulls over to the curb a few feet ahead of me and I hear Tavy's annoyed "So just where're you going, Benton?" that I remember the pizza article.

I brake my bike, red-faced. The wail of an electric guitar spills out from the van's speakers into the twilit air.

"Listen, you guys," I say. "I'm really sorry. I just...forgot."

Carl hops out and helps me lift the ten-speed into the van.

Settling into a seat next to Carl I apologize again.

"The girl," Keith cracks, "is obviously not into pizza."

"What can I say?"

"Nothing," Tavy said. "Forget it, Kara. We know you can be absent-minded."

"It happens to the best of us," Carl adds.

The radio tune ends and I hear a familiar howl and then a gravelly bass voice emanating from the van's speakers.

Aiee-ee-ee-ee-ee-owwww!
DAR-R-R-lin!!!
Awwww-right! That is one fine tune and comin' up in just a little while, we're gonna spin Neil Diamond's latest, but first we've gotta pay some bills, my friends, so here's a word from—

"Turn it off," I say.

"Hey, where's your loyalty?" Carl says. "That's your stepfather isn't it? Besides, he's good."

Tavy ignores Carl and presses a button to change the station. A strain of easy-listening music fills the car. Keith and Carl groan.

"I feel like I'm in a dentist's office," Carl moans.

"Carl," Tavy says, "just be quiet and think pizza."

By the time we reach Luigi's we are all really hungry, but as we scan the menu Tavy explains the rules of the Pizza War.

"We have to order the exact same thing at every place we try," she said. "Otherwise it won't be a fair contest. I think we should choose something standard—like pizza with three or four toppings."

"This sounds okay to me," Carl says, pointing to a cheese, pepperoni, green pepper, and mushroom combination, and then glancing at the rest of us for our opinion.

"What? No anchovies?" Keith protests. "No bacon rinds?"

Tavy and I groan.

"He's gotta be kidding," I say to Tavy.

"Uh-uh," Tavy says, shaking her head. "Keith is into exotic pizza. We have shared a lot of pizzas and the only topping I haven't seen him order has been Cheerios and shoelaces."

"They *have* Cheerios and shoelaces here?" Keith asks, with exaggerated hopefulness.

"Never mind," Tavy says. She exchanges greetings with the waitress who appears, order-pad at the ready. "We'll have one extra large pizza with cheese, pepperoni, green pepper, and mushroom," Tavy says. "And," she adds, turning to us, "I presume I may order a Coke for everyone?"

"Actually I was hoping for a banana-mint shake," Keith says. "However," he adds, noticing Tavy's scowl, "uh, in the interest of scientific accuracy I will have a Coke."

We eat our pizza, Tavy scribbling our comments in a notebook open next to her plate.

"By the way," I say casually, "I bumped into Reid Tyler after school today. He says he plans to join the *Eagle*."

"Yeah, I talked to him this afternoon myself," Keith says. "He showed me some of the stuff he did back in his school in Saginaw. Nice work. We're lucky to have him."

"He mentioned that he plans to join us at lunch in the Press Room," I add.

"I don't get it," Carl says. "I thought he was part of Dina's crowd."

"That assumption you made, Carl," I say, as ponderously as I can manage, "is a good example of what is called jumping to wrong conclusions. Obviously, Reid Tyler has a lot more character than you gave him credit for."

"Oh, let's face it," Tavy says. "The average person can only hang around with the fast-track bunch for so long before they realize that most of those kids have brains made of tapioca pudding."

Looking up from his pizza, Keith arches his eyebrows mock-hopefully. "They have tapioca pudding here?" he asks with an innocent grin.

"Well, aren't you glad you came?" Tavy asks me as Keith's van jounces up the gravel road to Strand House. Outside, the world is dark and fog-ridden, and a round moon dots the hazy sky, a giant pearl glowing through the mist. The van's headlights cut through the swirling darkness and Strand House finally looms over us.

"Pull up in back, Keith," I instructed him. "Then I can put my bike away on the verandah."

Keith pulls the van up to the steps of the verandah, and Carl helps me lug my ten-speed up the short flight of stairs.

"I guess nobody's home yet," I say, glancing up at the mansion's blackened windows. Mom's bridge night.

"Cripes," Carl says, as I fumble in my purse for my key, "isn't it kind of spooky being in a house this big all on your lonesome?"

"Carl," I say patiently, "I know I can always count on you to have a comforting word."

"Uh, sorry, Kara, I guess I put my foot in it, didn't I?"

"It's okay, Carl," I reply, making a conscious attempt to suppress the long-suffering tone from my voice.

"Uh, if you'd like, I could come in with you—until your Mom or Zack gets back. I can always call my dad to give me a ride home."

"No thanks, Carl," I say as I turn the key in the lock and slip in. "Good night."

I hear the van rumble off as I busy myself flicking on light switches in the corridor. Leave it to Carl to come up with an original line. Uh, your house looks haunted—want me to stay with you?

Of course, it's easier to be brave when all the corridor lights are blazing. The electric glare seems to chase away unsettling memories.

I am in the foyer and about to jog up the stairwell when I notice them on the white marble floor. I have seen them before, but familiarity does nothing to decrease the small stabbing feeling of unreality.

Footprints. Glistening and wet, they start at the oak doors and lead to the carpeted stairway.

Trembling, I bend down and touch the tips of my fingers to one of the wet marks on the floor. Cold. So cold. I shiver and try desperately to shake off the awful image that is forming in my mind.

Hold it, Kara. Control yourself, I tell myself. Put a cap on that imagination of yours. Just be logical and look for a rational explanation.

Beth. Beth had probably gone for a stroll, plowed through a puddle or two, and tracked this water over the foyer floor.

Except. Except that these were the kind of footprints a man's boots would leave, and Beth, whose feet were tiny, usually wore pumps with wedge heels. Except that Beth had left the house at five. Over three hours ago. Except that this is not the first time I've seen prints in the foyer.

Looking up into the velvety blackness at the head of the stairwell, I shiver again. Perhaps, I think, I should have taken Carl up on his offer. Taking a deep breath I flick the stairwell light on and deliberately start up the stairs to the second floor where my room is.

There has to be a rational explanation, I tell myself. If I think about it long enough it'll come to me. I will not allow myself to get spooked.

The house is quiet, unnaturally so. It is so silent that all I hear is the crickets outside and the sound of the wind cutting through the woods, a gentle mournful keening.

"Steady, Kara," I whisper softly to myself. And the wind somehow seems to echo. Ka-a-a-a-a-r-a-a-a.

Heart pounding despite myself, I plod quickly over the pale blue carpeting in the corridor and yank open the door to my room. Blackness. Silence.

With uncertain fingers I flick on the light switch. Nothing. Only the familiar clutter of my room. I turn on the black-and-white portable which is on my desk and soon the room is filled with a reassuring babble. New improved laundry detergents. Better cake mixes. Superb bargains from a local auto dealer. I let a slow sigh of relief shudder through me.

Maybe Mom's right, I think. About my letting myself be suggestible, allowing the stories I've heard about Strand House spark my imagination to work overtime.

I sit down on my cushioned window seat. Outside the world is a painting done with a palette of grays and blacks. From my window's vantage point I can see the moon overhanging the lake. Full and luminous it casts a diagonal bolt of light across the water like a path to another world. The little white housekeeper's cottage nearby shimmers ethereally. Propping my elbows up on the high sill of the casement windows, I rest my cheek against my forearm and watch Lantern Lake glittering through the thin mist that floats past the glass pane.

The footprints? I am the suggestible type, I tell myself. I have only imagined them. And the things that happened at the last full moon and the one before that—I imagined those, too. None of it is—or could be—real.

Soon my breathing becomes deep and more regular. A grayness blots out the world. The trees standing outside Strand House like silent sentinels, seem to echo my thoughts in the lulling rustle of their branches.

Re-e-e-e-e-a-al, they seem to murmur. Re-e-e-e-e-a-al.

Chapter Four

It's like being dizzy, I decide groggily, this off-balance feeling. Like being dizzy or half awake.

Is that what's happening, I wonder? Am I waking up?

Yes. Must be. Because here I am lifting my head from the window seat where I must have dozed off. Blinking I try to focus my gaze on the digital clock standing on my dresser. Even in the darkness the glowing red numerals are easy to read. Nine-forty.

Darkness? My mind shifts gears and thoughts start tumbling along one after another.

The light, the TV—someone has turned them off. Not Mom. She would have shaken me awake and made sure I went to bed. Who then?

I blink again as my eyes get used to the inky stillness. The moonlight pouring in through the window dimly outlines the shadowy forms in my room. The dresser, the bed, my desk, the couch, the end tables. All still and motionless.

Except.

Except for the dark shape that is somehow unfamiliar.

Suddenly my mouth goes dry and my lips begin to tremble. The words spill out in a harsh awkward whisper.

"Who—who is it?"

No answer. Only a slow movement of limbs. In the dim light I can see the figure stir.

"Who are you?" I ask, my voice trembling. "What do you want?"

The dim shape detaches itself from the shadows and advances, a silvery form in the semi-light. Vaporish and wavering as a mirage, he approaches and I can barely make out the pale features, the hair matted down with moisture. Eyes of no particular shade look at me—but through me as well.

He raises his hand.

I scream.

"Kara! What is it?"

Mom and Beth are at the door. The lights are on and the TV is blaring.

"I—I—"

"Sweetheart," Mom says, "you're white as a sheet. What on earth...?"

I blink up into Mom's face. "Mom," I ask, "did you turn the light on?"

"No, Kara," Mom says, slightly puzzled by my question. "It was on when we came in. Now tell me what happened? You didn't—have that dream again, did you?"

"What dream?" Beth asks.

"Well, since we moved into Strand House, Kara's had a few nightmares. Now tell me, Kara, is that what happened?"

"You're right, Mom," I say. "It was just a nightmare."

"And no wonder," Mom says. "Going off to sleep watching stuff like this." She nods over at the TV where Lon Chaney, Jr., under the influence of a full moon, is undergoing a dramatic transformation into a werewolf.

Mom gives me an off-center smile as she presses the TV's off button. "From now on nothing but documentaries for you."

"Right," I concur. What else can I tell her? I know that whatever I say will only add to her belief that I'm letting my imagination run away with me.

"Now, why don't you change into your pj's, get into bed, and get a proper night's sleep?"

"Sure, Mom."

Mom touches my cheek in a quick, reassuring gesture and leaves, closing the door behind her.

"Okay, now level with me, Kara," Beth says. "*What* is going on here?"

I blink innocently up at Beth.

"What do you mean?" I ask.

"Oh, c'mon, Kara," she says, a little irritably. "I know you like the back of my hand. You might be able to fob Mom off with that nightmare story, but there's something you aren't telling us, isn't there?"

Despite the fact that I am still a bit shaken up by the events of moments ago I can't help but feel a little amused.

"Why, Beth, what more could there possibly be to talk about? I mean, I thought I was the only Benton for miles around with a runaway imagination."

She stares at me intently for a moment, then looks away, biting her lip.

"Beth," I say slowly, the playfulness vanishing from my voice, "you've seen something too."

She wraps her arms around herself and nods nervously.

"This afternoon—as I was leaving the house. In the foyer..." She pauses for a long moment and then the words come out in a faint whisper. "Footprints."

I nod. "I've seen them, too."

"But, Kara, there was no one here. No one could have made those tracks."

"Have you told Mom?"

She shakes her head. "You know how she is about things like that."

"Do I know?" I sigh. "Mom's a doll but she's got a block as far as psychic phenomena go. Tell her about mysterious footprints, and she'll hand you a rag and a bucket, suggesting that you mop them up."

"Or trace the source," Beth giggles.

"Straight back into the lake," I add. It helps, for some reason, to be outrageous.

"Kara," Beth says, suddenly sobering, "you don't think there really is a ghost, do you?"

I shrug and turn to look out the window. But I'm obviously not as good at hiding things as I think I am.

"You *do*," Beth says. "You've seen something haven't you, Kara?"

Grudgingly I look up at her and nod.

"This is the third time," I say.

"*What?* What did you see?"

"A man," I say. "A hazy form. He was— glistening wet."

Beth shivers. "Oh, Kara, how *creepy*."

"Creepy is the operative word," I agree.

"But who? Why?"

"And those are the operative questions," I say. "Unfortunately I have no answers. All I know is that ever since we moved into Strand House it's been like this—whenever the moon is full the fireworks go off."

Beth collapsed onto the couch in a shudder. "Then it's true," she says.

"What's true?"

"About Strand House being haunted."

"I don't know," I reply, shrugging. "You see, I've got this overactive imagination."

"Be serious, Kar."

"Well, I am being serious, Beth. Look, Mom absolutely refuses to listen when I tell her about the stuff I've seen. And I'm not one hundred percent sure I'm seeing things. I mean, I seem to recall that I left the light on and the TV going when I dozed off. When my nocturnal visitor dropped by, however, the room was absolutely still. And then, when I screamed, suddenly the light and the TV were back on. Now doesn't that sound to you as though there's a good possibility I dreamed it all?"

"And did you dream this, too?" Beth says, standing up suddenly and pointing to her feet. Her face is bloodless as she stares down at the varnished parquet floor.

Gazing down I see them—a watery track leading from the door to about three feet away from me. Footprints.

The mood at the breakfast table on Saturday morning is subdued. Nobody does much talking and Zack's few attempts at sparking a conversation are dying quiet deaths.

Serves him right, I think, unsympathetic to his discomfort. I have come to actively dislike the fake heartiness he has taken to projecting lately. It might work over the airwaves, Zack, but it won't work on me. Why can't you be real, I wonder, the way you were when you were dating Mom a few months back? Why do you have to be so tense and phony these days?

I glance over at Zack. He is wearing his usual gear—open-collared plaid shirt, jeans, and a suede vest. Tense or not he *is* attractive, I realize, and it's not difficult to see why Mom fell for him. With his large amber eyes that tilt up at the outer corners and his ash-blond hair that stands away from his face like a shaggy mane, he looks lionlike and, though I hate to admit it, almost noble.

But I can tell, although Beth's doing her best to hide it, that she's disappointed with Zack, too. It's too bad, I think cynically, that Beth didn't get to know him before the wedding. He *had* been different then—warm, funny, and real. It's incredible to remember it now, but I actually had liked him back then. Before he turned into such a phony and put up all these superficial walls.

Our conversational exchanges continue to move in fits and starts, and sputter out in several places. And, when Zack finally gets up and announces that he has an appointment with his accountant, Beth appears to be as relieved as I am.

Mom gives Zack a peck on the cheek, and he disappears up the stairwell.

"Girls," Mom says quietly as we begin to clear the dishes, "couldn't you have tried a little harder to keep a conversation going with your stepfather? He does want so awfully badly to get along with you two."

I know I won't get anywhere with Mom by telling her what a phony I think Zack is, and so I ask her, rather abruptly, the question that's been preying on my mind all morning.

"Mom, why did he buy Strand House?"

"What?"

"Why did he buy this place? I mean, was there a reason?"

"Well, let me see. Oh, yes, I seem to recall that we did talk about this place during that interview I did with him for the *Herald*. Remember that?"

How could I forget? It was the interview that had brought them together.

"I seem to recall Zack's telling me that the mansion had been a super-bargain. Something about its former owner willing to let it go for a song."

"I wonder why?" Beth comments dryly, stacking cups and saucers and carrying them to the dishwasher. Predictably, Mom fails to catch the ironic tone in Beth's voice.

"Oh, I'm not sure but there have always been a few silly stories circulating to the effect that Strand House is—" She breaks off, looking in my direction.

"Haunted?" Beth supplies.

"Now, girls," Mom says, "people are always making up stories about places with exotic histories. As a matter of fact, I think it was rather shrewd of Zack to buy this place. He not only got a super-bargain but living in a so-called haunted house rather suits that offbeat radio personality of his. But," she continues impatiently, "you girls should know better than to give credence to those old stories. After all, this is the twentieth century we're living in. And Strand House is set in a beautiful stretch of Michigan lake property, not in a forest in Transylvania. Right?"

"Absolutely," Beth says, her voice ringing with quiet irony.

"No question, Mom," I say resignedly.

But, just out of curiosity, I want to add, where do we keep the wooden stakes and the silver bullets?

An hour later I go upstairs to watch Mom paint. She paints in the studio she's set up in one of the third-floor rooms. Mom's studio is the only room on the third floor that's actually used for anything. The rest stand empty or are storage areas for odds and ends.

She's standing at her easel working on a view of Lantern Lake as I enter the studio. With a quick, deft movement her brush flecks the blue water on her canvas with sparkling highlights.

"Nice work, Mom."

"Thanks, Kara." Mom smiles up at me.

"Tavy called, Mom. We're going skating."

"Fine, dear," Mom mumbles vaguely, dabbing streaks of sunlight onto a wisp of cloud.

A few minutes later I hear Tavy's Jeep roll up the drive. I grab my skates and dash out the front door into the midmorning sunshine.

"Wow," Tavy says as I settle into my seat. "Talk about eager beavers. You came out like a shot out of a cannon. What's up?"

I feel my face flush a little as she navigates the semicircle of drive, turning onto the gravel road leading away from Strand House.

"Well, remember what I told you about last month?" I ask quietly.

"Wow," she says turning her head excitedly toward me, swerving one of the Jeep's front wheels off the gravel track in the process.

"Hey, watch it, Tav."

"Sorry," she says, turning her attention back to the road. "It's just that it's kind of exciting. Kara, you've got to give me all the details."

Tavy believes completely in the local legends about Strand House. One of her uncles, a corporate attorney, spent a night in the housekeeper's cottage several years ago as part of a fraternity initiation ritual. According to Tavy, something happened in the cottage that convinced her uncle he never wanted to lay eyes on Strand House or its environs again.

I tell Tavy about the previous evening's goings on as we tool down Orchard Trail. She lets out a low whistle as I complete my narrative.

"No wonder you came barreling out of there this morning. I think if it were me I would have barreled out last night and stayed out. How are you ever going to be able to spend another night there?"

"I'll be okay, Tavy," I say soberly. "Somehow, weird as it all was, I didn't feel threatened."

"But, Kara, you said he was pointing—at you." She shudders.

"I'm not saying I wasn't scared. I was, believe me. It's just that I didn't feel as though I was in any danger."

"Of course not—you were probably in shock. Kara, do you think it was...Jack Strand?"

"I don't know, Tavy," I answer, staring at the birches and maples whizzing past us. "Whoever it is, he's not much of a conversationalist."

A few minutes later we arrive at the doors of the ice arena.

It feels good to be at the arena with Tavy. Besides being fun it feels normal and ordinary and reassuring. If I make an effort, I feel I can almost force myself to forget about last night's events.

Tavy and I took skating lessons together a couple of years back, and Tavy insists that I'm a terrific skater. The truth is that neither of us is anywhere near competitive caliber. But my spins and jumps are pretty good, and I can do a passable free-skating routine. I guess that skating, to me, is the same as painting is to Mom: a place where I can let myself go.

I sit on a scarred wooden bench, pull off my Adidas, and tug on my Silver Stars. I am finished lacing my left skate when, without warning, a small pair of arms wraps around my neck.

"Kara!" a familiar voice says. I look up and see Nikki Marsh.

"Nikki! Hello. Are you learning to skate?"

Her head bobs up and down so enthusiastically her red knit cap seems in danger of falling off. "Uh-huh. I got new skates and everything. See," she adds with a grin, pointing down at her feet.

"So how are you doing?" I ask.

The uncertain expression on Nikki's face tells me exactly how things are going.

"Well," Nikki says. "I can stand up on the ice...sometimes."

"Is anyone helping you, Nikki?" I ask gently.

She shakes her head no. "I take lessons every Monday with Lisa. She's my structure."

"Your instructor?"

"That's what I said. Lisa's not here today."

"Well, then who brought you?"

"Reid and his girl friend. Mom and Dad are in Chicago and my baby sitter got sick this morning..."

At the mention of Reid's name I feel a nervous little pull at my heart. So Reid was here...with his *girl friend*!

A pair of red pompomed skates is clomping toward me on the rubber matting of the arena lobby.

"What's holding you up, Kar?" It's Tavy.

"Tavy, this is Nikki. She's one of the children I work with at the center."

Tavy nods a greeting over to Nikki, who giggles in reply.

"So are you ready to go skating?" Tavy asks.

"I'll be with you in a little while, Tav. I want to give Nikki here a few pointers."

Tavy shrugs good-naturedly and heads to the ice.

"How many lessons did you say you've had, Nikki?" I ask.

"One," Nikki answers.

Sighing, I help her balance her way over the matting and into the arena.

Fifteen minutes later, Nikki is lit up like a Christmas tree as she finds her blades making small independent gliding motions over the ice. As I'm congratulating her, a pair of silver blades snowplow stop a few feet ahead of us. The skater turns to face us, and I look up into Reid Tyler's face.

"Hi," he says, his smile polite and formal.

"Hi, Reid," I answer. Up close his eyes are an incredible blue. He's wearing jeans and a navy wool sweater which nicely complements the ruddy coloring of his complexion.

"Reid, *look*. I'm *skating*," Nikki shouts. She moves a hesitant glide forward, arms flailing.

Reid laughs. "Hey, that's great, Nikko," he says, and then turns to me. "Listen, Kara, thanks for helping Nikki out. Dina and I appreciate it."

When he mentions Dina he nods over to the side of the rink. For the first time since he appeared in front of me, my vision clears enough to focus on individuals other than Reid. Sure enough, Dina is standing only a few feet away. Dressed in a snazzy and obviously expensive lavender wool sweater and pants, with a matching lavender tam perched atop her head, she looks almost too chic for a skating rink full of high school kids.

I smile at her and she returns my overture with a cool noncommittal smile of her own. It's probably prejudice on my part, but for some reason fashion queens never strike me as the kind of people five-year-olds can spend a fun afternoon with.

"Gee, Reid, I'm having fun with Nikki," I say. "Why don't you and Dina go ahead and skate, and I'll watch Nikki for a little while longer."

"That'd be great, Kara. I appreciate it. You know, I thought I'd have to cancel my skating date this morning after Nikki's baby sitter called in sick, but after I explained the situation to Dina she suggested we simply take Nikki along. She's a great girl. Really loves kids."

I'll bet, I think to myself as I watch Dina ignore Nikki's faltering attempts to skate over in her direction.

As I watch Reid skate off with Dina, his gloved hand closing over hers, there is a tightness in my throat that hurts. Had I actually thought, when Reid made his appearance at the center, that he might become interested in me the same way he was interested in Dina?

Nikki's hand tugging at my sleeve distracts me from my dreary train of thought.

"Kara, can you show me some fancy skating?"

"I could show you a few figures, but you're not ready to do them yet."

"I just want to watch you. Okay?"

"Why not?" I sigh. Doing a few routines will get my mind off Reid anyway. "Stay by the arena wall and watch."

It's funny but the ice is one place where I feel absolutely un-self-conscious. I guess that's because I know I'm never going to skate competitively. I feel loose and free as I go through all the routines I've learned in my skating classes—the spins and jumps and Mohawks.

I'm almost finished and I feel pleasantly winded. I wind down from a quick drop-spin, and when I come to a complete stop I find myself staring, across a few short yards of air space, into a pair of familiar blue eyes.

It's Reid. He's standing outside the arena, leaning on the railing, and there's a look on his face I can't decipher. For a moment I have the odd sensation that we're going to exchange glances forever.

But that, I tell myself, is ridiculous. And, sure enough, a moment later Dina is tugging impatiently at his sleeve, and he turns to go.

Chapter Five

He likes you, Kara."

It's Saturday evening and Tavy has felt the need to call and assure me that Reid Tyler is madly in love with me.

"Oh, c'mon, Tav. Be serious."

"I am being serious. What's it going to take to convince you? An engraved announcement?"

"Hmmmm," I consider. "That would be a nice touch."

"Okay." She sighs exasperatedly. "Believe what you want. But one day I'm going to be able to say 'I told you so.'"

"Beth left for the U this afternoon," I say, eager to get off the subject of me and my killer effect on men.

"Kara! She didn't leave you alone in that place, did she?"

"What do you mean *alone*? Of course not. Mom and Zack are here."

"I know. But neither of them knows about— you know."

I sigh. "Well, to tell you the truth, I practically had to pack Beth's bags for her. I guess she felt the same way you do about my being left to my own devices."

"Couldn't she have stayed a little longer?"

"What difference would it make, Tav? The weird things that happen around here happen no matter who's in the house. Besides, I told you I don't honestly feel as though there's any danger."

"Kara Benton," she says incredulously, "you have nerves of steel."

"Actually I think they're made out of some sort of aluminum alloy."

"*Kara*," Tavy warns, an edge of laughter creeping into her remonstration.

"Okay, okay, nerves of steel," I concur. "So far I've got the allure of Mata Hari and the guts of General Patton—"

"And the obstinacy of a mule."

"Tavy!"

"Well, it's true. You can be angry with me if you want, but I think this stiff upper lip approach of yours is all wrong. You need help."

"I'm not saying I don't agree with you, Tavy. But who, exactly, am I supposed to turn to? You can count out my Mom. The idea of asking Zack for help totally turns me off. And that narrows it down to me, myself, and the local ghosthunters' society. And, for your information, there is no local ghosthunters' society."

"I just don't like the idea of your facing this alone," Tavy counters.

"Neither do I," I say, my inflection wry. "Seriously, though, Tav, I'm pretty sure there's nothing to worry about. I mean, if the apparition were going to harm me it would have done so by now."

"Then what does it want?"

"I wish I knew. You don't know how much I wish I knew."

Ending the conversation with her, I replace the receiver on the cradle and then snuggle back against the couch in my room, wrapping the maize-and-blue afghan Grandma Benton sent me last Christmas around myself. I shiver in spite of its woolly warmth.

My eyes travel to the large casement windows that overlook the lake. The sky over the lake is an oppressive gray—twilight mingled with the threat of rain. The water, reflecting the sky, is leaden, and the wind from the north sends foaming whitecaps crashing against the sandy shores at the base of the hill.

I try to think calmly about the ghost. There has to be some reason for this reappearing apparition. But what?

Tavy's right, I realize. I do need someone to share this with. It's impossible for me to make sense of it all on my own. How can I? Every time I recall the things I've seen I end up shuddering, my mind skittering away from any sort of logical analysis. I have to find someone who can help me. But who?

No answer.

I prop my head against the arm of the couch and immediately fall into a fitful sleep. And then I have an odd dream: I feel that I'm out in the gray evening, walking through the mist that swirls over the shores of Lantern Lake.

I feel confused and frightened. Bewildered. But a figure is coming toward me. And I know, even before it reaches me, who it is and that I needn't be frightened. And then he's beside me, Reid, his warm fingers wrapping over mine. And suddenly the world isn't gray anymore.

Monday morning, sitting through Mr. Berrien's history class, I feel impatient as a five-year-old on a birthday morning—impatient with Mr. Berrien, history in general, and the rise of the Roman republic in particular.

It's funny because Mr. B is not a bad teacher and I enjoyed his classes last week. But today it's just impossible to concentrate. I stare at dates on the board, but they blur and fade as I find myself remembering the way Reid skated at the rink, the lithe movement of his body over the ice.

Wake up, Kara, I command myself. You've got it bad.

Well, that's the kind of luck I have, I decide. When my Mom marries a famous DJ, he turns out to be a world-class phony who lives in a haunted mansion. When I fall for a guy who is my idea of terminally neat, he turns out to be just about going steady with a future editor of *Vogue*.

The late bell rang ten minutes ago, and my eyes keep traveling like magnets to Reid's seat—which is still empty. I notice Larry Gelhorn's and Brad Hamell's seats are as well. I wonder if Mr. Berrien's eyes, flicking over the empty places, notice the pattern—all three of the guys are in Dina's crowd.

I wonder where Reid is, whether he's sick, or whether the absence of the other guys is an indication that the three of them are goofing off together.

Sure enough—at eight-fifty they walk in, Brad, Larry, and Reid. I can tell by the crease in

Mr. Berrien's forehead that he doesn't appreciate his class being interrupted.

"Sorry, Mr. Berrien," Brad explains. "Reid had car trouble, and Larry and I stopped to help him."

"Take your seats. I'll talk to you three after class," Mr. Berrien says curtly as he continues to chalk names and dates on the board for us to copy into our notebooks. It is obvious from his manner that he has doubts about Brad's version of events.

For the benefit of the class, Brad drops his jaw in an exaggerated display of offended innocence just before he turns around to slip into his seat. I see him catch Larry's eye and give him a quick conspiratorial wink.

At this particular moment Brad Hamell and Larry Gelhorn are not exactly my favorite people. I have known them almost as long as I have known Carl, and the two of them have always been goof-offs. Still, goof-offs or not, they're part of Dina's crowd and they're now influencing Reid to act like an airhead, too.

I am on the verge of being angry at Reid, too, for being so easily led, when, as he's settling into his seat, he turns around, catches my eye, and smiles.

Talk about incredible moments. Suddenly Brad and Larry are the furthest things from my mind. I can hardly concentrate on Mr. Berrien's lecture, and when he asks us to take out a sheet of loose-leaf paper for a short essay quiz on the history of ancient Greece, I have to think twice before I can remember dates and places.

My concentration hardly improves when, about five minutes after the late arrivals have settled into their seats, we hear a wild shriek from down the hall. Naturally Mr. Berrien leaves to find out just what is happening. When he returns he is wearing a weary expression and, although he addresses everyone in the class, it's pretty clear that he's particularly aiming his message at Reid, Larry, and Brad.

"Whoever the party or parties are," he says, "who put the garter snakes into Bonnie Patson's desk in biology class, you'll be glad to know that they were discovered about a minute ago and Bonnie's recovering."

From where I'm sitting I can see Larry fighting to suppress a grin. I feel vaguely sick. This was a typical Larry-and-Brad space-cadet antic—they love to needle kids like Bonnie, who has a reputation at Lakeview for being a screamer.

But why had Reid gone along with the stupid joke?

When the bell rings the end of class Reid, Brad, and Larry cluster around Mr. Berrien's desk. They are wearing expressions just sober enough to fake Mr. Berrien out. They obviously have decided to play it innocent.

I try to understand how it is when you're in a group—how you have to go along with some dumb things sometimes.

It doesn't work.

As terrific as Reid is I can't overlook the fact that he's letting himself be led by guys that make the Three Stooges look brilliant. It's painful to admit it to myself, but I feel my respect for Reid fly out the window.

Out in the hallway I'm waylaid by Glenda Reiker, a fellow sophomore and Lakeview High's unofficial social director. She obviously has no way of assessing the moods of her potential enlistees. She wants to know if I'll serve on the homecoming dance committee. At this moment in time I'm not quite sure I'll ever smile again, let alone dance or serve on a festive committee.

Still, it takes me a good three minutes before I can convince her there's no room in my schedule for additional extracurricular activities. Glenda spots Tavy sailing down the hall and sallies after her with a determined glint in her eye, barely bothering to sign off.

I move along, hoping I won't be too late for algebra. But before I get there I hear footsteps catching up to mine in the now nearly deserted hallway.

"So how's it going, Kara?"

I look up at the handsome face set with the knock-em-dead eyes, and sigh softly. Only an hour ago, I think, I would have been thrilled by Reid's attention. Now, however, I find myself responding coolly.

"Oh, okay," I answer.

The smile on his face vanishes like an ember cooling to gray and his manner becomes more formal.

"I guess I just wanted to thank you again for watching Nikki for me."

"No problem," I say, with equal formality. "I enjoyed it."

"Right," he says. "Well, I guess I'll see you in the Press Room then. At lunch, I mean."

"What? Oh, right," I say.

And he turns and walks away, his gait easy and graceful.

What is it with me anyway? I ask myself. For weeks I'd wanted Reid to notice me. And yet, when he finally does, I give him the cold shoulder. Am I being too hard on him for going along with Brad and Larry?

No.

No, the part of me that always has the right answers replies. The Reid I'd fallen for wouldn't be into grammar-school antics. He wouldn't let himself be led by a couple of airheads.

As painful as it is to admit it to myself, I have to realize I'd fallen for a Reid that didn't exist.

And then an ugly and cruel thought forms in my head. Of course Reid likes me. How hard could it be to catch the attention of a guy who let types like Brad and Larry do his thinking for him?

I watch as Reid's tall lean figure disappears around a bend in the corridor.

I shouldn't feel anything, I tell myself. I've followed my gut feelings, haven't I? I shouldn't feel bad about what I've done, only relieved. Right?

But, for some reason, it's not that easy.

Chapter Six

When Reid walks into the Press Room with Keith, the two of them are yakking away together as though they'd known each other all of their lives. Keith introduces Reid around. When it's my turn to say hello I smile weakly in Reid's direction and he nods rather gravely in response.

I notice Tavy, who is sitting at Mrs. Ferris's desk, take in our exchange, her eyes narrowing like a cat's. I make a mental note to prepare for the third degree that I know is sure to come.

I don't have to wait long.

The bell rings and Tavy and I are on our way to English class when she springs the question.

"Kara, what happened?"

"What happened?" I ask innocently. "Oh, you mean at Strand House last night? Nothing actually. It was a very quiet—"

"*Kara*," she pleads, "you know what I mean. What happened to the crush of the century?"

I sober up. "I guess Carl was right, Tavy," I say. "Reid's definitely not my type. It just took me awhile to realize it, that's all."

"You've got to be kidding."

"I'm dead serious."

"Well, Kara, I wish I'd have known about this big switcheroo this morning."

"Why?"

"Because Carl told me he can't make it to the pizza-rating dinner tonight—he has debate-team practice—and I lined someone else up to sub for him. Guess who?"

"Oh, no."

"That's right," she says. "Reid Tyler. I thought at the time that it was a great idea."

I sigh. "Don't worry about it, Tav. I can handle it. And, listen, I know you meant well. It's not your fault I'm fickle."

"Fickle is one thing," she counters. "Foolish is another."

"Tav!"

"Kara, Reid is one neat guy. You two would make a great team."

Sure, I think. I could make the cream pies and he could ram them in people's faces. No thanks.

The atmosphere at the Pizza Corner restaurant is warm and collegiate, pennants and photos of sports teams from nearby Lakeview Community College bedecking its brick walls. A candle flickers inside a red glass globe in the center of our table, casting an ebb and flow of gentle light over Reid's face as he talks with Keith.

I guess Tavy has realized by now that she has nothing to worry about as far as Reid and I are concerned. The meal has proceeded uneventfully with each of us quite happily ignoring the other.

At seven-fifteen the restaurant loudspeakers crackle to life and a familiar voice blasts out.

...and welcome to WHWL, my friends. This is your old pal, Zack Morris, here. We're gonna roll some tapes and rap awhile. But just now, in honor of a holiday that is fast approaching and which, DAR-R-R-lin, just happens to be one of my favorite days of the year—Halloween—we are gonna play an old, old tune. This was requested by Jojo Regal of Lakeview High. Way to go, Jojo!
Aiee-ee-ee-ee-ee-ee-owwww!

Tavy gets up and drags a protesting Keith along with her to the small dance floor in back of the restaurant. Soon they are both gyrating to the beat of "The Monster Mash."

"It must be kind of interesting," Reid says, "having a DJ for a stepfather."

"Yeah, I guess so," I reply with deliberate curtness.

"I mean Zack seems like a together person."

"Does he?" I ask coolly, my eyes traveling to the pictures on the brick walls.

Reid's hand slapping down on the wooden table makes me jump.

"Okay," he begins, his voice cold, "you know something, Kara? I've had it. Talk about hot and cold. What are you? One of those girls who likes to tease?"

I guess I must look as hurt as I feel because the next thing I know Reid is standing up and pushing his chair in, his face flushed.

"Look," he says, "I'm sorry, Kara. I—I guess I overreacted. It's just that I—well, I thought we could be friends."

"Reid, sit down," I say softly.

Reid's mouth hardens into an unsmiling line. "Are you sure you can stand another moment of my obviously repellent company?"

I sigh. "Your company is definitely not repellent. And...you're right. We can be friends."

Of course we can. Not boyfriend/girlfriend. But friends.

Who was I, after all, to be so judgmental about him? I'd imagined this perfect guy and made him fit the bill. And then when it became clear that the Reid I'd thought I'd seen was only a product of my imagination, I'd set myself up as judge and jury and sentenced him to my own personal icing out.

Wasn't that playing the very same game I disliked Dina and her crowd for playing: setting up personal standards for others, then giving them the cold shoulder when they didn't, or couldn't, match up.

"Reid...I'm sorry."

He sits down, looking at me thoughtfully.

"Apology accepted," he says finally, then adds with a small smile, "Care to drink on it?"

"Why not?"

We clink our Coke glasses together and sip.

"Want to talk about it?" he asks.

What can I tell him? That I think his friends Brad and Larry are low-lifes? What's the point?

"I—there have been things happening in my life lately."

"Yes?"

"Odd things. It's—they're hard to explain. I mean how do you explain..."

There is a small silence and then Reid supplies the word, his voice soft. "A ghost?"

The word falls between us with the startling impact of a glass breaking.

"T-Tavy told you."

Reid nods.

"You probably think I'm certifiable."

He puts one index finger on the rim of his Coke glass, tracing the outline of the lip.

"No," he says.

"Look, don't cater to me," I protest.

"Who's catering?" he returns.

"Look, Reid, don't tell me that *you* believe in ghosts."

"I believe in possibilities," he says.

"You don't have to pretend to make me feel better."

"Kara," Reid says, an edge of exasperation in his tone, "give me credit for a little character, won't you? If I'm telling you I believe it's possible that something odd is going on at Strand House, that's exactly what I mean."

I can feel my cheeks reddening. Privately, character was exactly what I wasn't giving Reid credit for.

"I—I'm—"

"You're sorry. I know." His face hardens melodramatically, and I can tell he is fighting hard not to smile. "Well sorry isn't good enough, Kara. The only way I can see my way to forgiving you is—if you dance the next dance with me."

"I guess I have no choice." I sigh, with an equally melodramatic air of resignation, as the strains of "Evergreen" fill the restaurant.

"Absolutely none."

"All right then," I say, following him out onto the floor. "Anything for friendship, right?"

"Just keep believing in possibilities," Reid answers as his arm circles my waist and we begin to move with the music.

After Reid drops Keith and Tavy off he turns to me in the semidarkness of the car. "Kara, can we stop by my house for a while?" he asks. "There's something I want to show you."

I glance at the car clock. It's almost ten o'clock.

"I don't know, Reid. It's getting kind of late for a school night."

"If I promise to get you home by eleven?" he asks.

"I'll have to call Mom and tell her why I'm late."

Reid nods.

"You don't live too far from us," I comment as he tools his blue Camaro into a garage stall. We exit the garage and walk over the grassy lawn that separates the Tylers' split-level from the sandy shores of Lantern Lake.

"See," I say, pointing across the dark water to the hill that rises on the southwestern end of the lake. "There's Strand House."

A westerly wind blows steadily from over the lake, whipping my thin jacket almost off my shoulders. I start to shiver with the sudden chill. And then Reid is behind me, wrapping his long arms around me. I turn around to protest, but then his lips are touching mine, pressing gently down. I pull away.

"Reid," I say, "I'm sorry. I—I don't feel that way about you."

Near me there is a sound like a ragged sigh. But maybe it's just the wind shaking through the birches.

"Sorry," Reid says a moment later, his tone light, "but I've never been able to resist a pretty girl by moonlight."

"I have a simple solution to your problem," I counter. "Let's go indoors."

"After you, Miss Benton," he says, making a small flourish with his hand.

After exchanging greetings with Reid's parents and then calling my mother, I follow Reid to the rec room. There's a fire in the fireplace that seems on the verge of dying. Reid opens the glass and mesh screens and throws on another piece of wood. The dry wood crackles and snaps, and soon flames are dancing high, casting a flickering orange light over Reid and me.

"I really am sorry—about out there, Kara," he says. "It—it won't happen again."

"It's all right," I say.

"No, it isn't. I mean, you made it pretty clear to me earlier today that you're only interested in a friendship, not anything else. Listen, Kara, I think you're a pretty neat person to have as a friend."

The fireplace is giving off a warmth that melts away the chill of the outdoors. I sink down onto the rust corduroy sofa facing the fire. He leaves the room for a moment and returns with an envelope in his hands. I recognize it as the sort of envelope developers use to package snapshots.

"I took these pictures on Lantern Lake over the summer," he says, sitting down next to me and flipping the envelope open. "I didn't get around to having them developed until about two weeks ago."

He withdraws a stack of three-by-five prints and hands them over to me. I flip through the pictures, wondering what the point is. Most of the pictures are of Dina and her crowd swimming, boating, and water-skiing on Lantern Lake. Is he trying to let me know he had a great time over the summer?

Funny, I think, he never struck me as the insecure, braggy type.

"Well, what do you think?" he asks.

"Uh, very nice, Reid," I say. "I guess you had a lot of fun over the summer."

He looks at me witheringly.

"Kara, you didn't really look at these, did you?"

Who wanted to see two-dozen assorted snaps of Dina in two-dozen assorted bikinis? I wanted to shout at him. Instead I just hand the stack of photos back to him without a word. Reid takes them and stands up.

"Come here," he says, walking over to the billiard table standing in one corner of the room.

He flicks on the overhead light, and then starts spreading the photos out over the green felt surface like playing cards.

"Now look at them," he says. "Look carefully. Do you notice anything?"

Reluctantly I scan the pictures. And then I realize what Reid is trying to get me to notice.

One is a picture of Dina water-skiing past the stretch of lake-front that I recognize as my home territory. Behind Dina, Strand House provides a picturesque backdrop. The second photo is of the same stretch of lake, but there are no figures in the foreground.

"These pictures?" I ask, pointing to the two snapshots.

Reid nods.

"I took those shots around twilight," Reid says, pointing to one of the snaps. "That's when

I saw it. I was sure I was seeing things. That's why I took the second picture. Look at them.''

I pick up the two pictures and study them. The hazy shape is clearly visible in both pictures: a figure in the window of the housekeeper's cottage. In the second photo the figure is still in the window, although it seems to have shifted so that it's only partly visible at the edge of the window frame, as though it were walking away.

A shiver passed through me.

"I know what you mean," Reid says. "It gave me the creeps, too. But it *is* hazy and indefinite. It could just be a patch of mist."

"Yeah," I say sarcastically, "or a low-flying cloud."

Reid ignores me patiently. "But the way that it moved," he says, thinking out loud.

Ignoring him in return I continue my protest. "Just a flaw in the film," I insist, a half-smile playing on my lips.

"It isn't that," he says. "I went back to the developer and showed him the negatives. He insists they weren't damaged during processing."

"Then what's your conclusion, Sherlock?" I ask.

"I was hoping you could provide me with one," Reid says.

"Sorry," I counter. "I'm fresh out of conclusions."

"Kara, don't you ever trust your instincts?"

Sure, I think to myself. The same instincts that told me you were different from the rest of Dina's crowd. Still, his words strike close to home.

"Look, I know I'm not being all that brave about this, Reid, but what do you expect me to do? Make it public knowledge that Strand House is—"

"Haunted?" he supplies. "I thought that *was* public knowledge. I've heard stories about the place."

"Is that why you were ready with your camera?"

"No. It just happened."

"And I suppose you've made the pictures public knowledge?"

He breaks eye contact with me. "As a matter of fact, no, I haven't."

"I guess *your* gut feelings warned you that reporting ghostly visitations isn't exactly the sort of activity that gives an objective reporter high credibility."

"Okay," Reid concedes, "I get your drift. But I'm not asking you to go shout whatever you know about Strand House from the rooftops. I'm just asking you to level with *me* We're supposed to be friends, remember?"

The firelight casts an unsteady glow over Reid's face, but even in the uncertain light I can see sincerity in the depths of his eyes.

"Why is it so important to you, Reid?"

Reid sighs impatiently and begins gathering up the photographs from the billiard table.

"Honestly?" he asks. "I don't know. But maybe it's because it's the first time I've personally encountered something like this. To tell you the truth, Kara, I'm the Tyler family skeptic. A believer in facts and figures, if you will. I think that's one of the reasons I'm going to be a terrific investigative journalist someday—I don't accept anything on face value. I like to dig and get to the truth.

"Now, you take a person like me and tell me some place is haunted and I'll laugh in your face because chances are you haven't got a shred of evidence to substantiate your story. No facts.

"But these pictures are facts. And because they're facts they're a puzzle. They go against what I would generally believe to be true about the physical world—that you don't, as a rule, see ghosts rambling around old houses on summer twilights.

"In short, what we've got here is a first-rate mystery, and, for your information, crack investigative reporter types find mysteries irresistible.

"Uh, besides which," Reid continues, "you have friends who are concerned about you and who asked me if I could help."

"Tavy?"

He nods. "She told me about it when she stopped to help me last Monday. That was when my car went out of commission on the way to school and—"

"Wait a minute, Reid. Hold it. Say that again."

He looks at me curiously and repeats his statement.

"But—that was the day you came into world history with Brad and Larry. I thought you were—"

A frown creases Reid's brow and then, a moment later, he laughs.

"Goofing off with them? I'm sorry to disappoint you, Kara, but garter snakes are not my thing—especially not when they're planted in some poor kid's desk. Those guys saw me heading for class late, asked me what happened, and then just decided it would get them off the hook if they told Mr. B that they'd stopped to help me—unfortunately, I guess the two of them are unconvincing liars."

"But I thought—"

"Yeah, I can see what you thought. Gosh, thanks for the good opinion," he says wryly. "But I guess I shouldn't be too hard on you. Mr.

B didn't believe me until I offered to call the gas station and have him speak with the manager.''

"I—I'm sorry, Reid."

"Honest mistake." He smiles. "Forget it, Kara. Anyway, Tavy thinks that together we could get to the bottom of the goings-on at Strand House. And," he adds, gazing soberly at me, "I think we could, too." He pauses. "Now, are you going to level with me, Kara? What exactly did I see?"

I turn away from Reid and stare into the crackling fire, arms folded.

"What did you see? I don't know. I'm not sure. But it might have been a ghost."

We are both silent for a moment, staring into the dancing flames in the fireplace. But the silence is filled with a quiet understanding. I sense that Reid is with me, that come what may at Strand House I have an ally.

More than that, the wonderful realization begins to sink in that Reid had no part in Brad and Larry's sick joke, and didn't that mean that I had been right about Reid all along? In my mind I'm formulating the words, the best way to tell him what I want to say—that now I know that he doesn't share Brad and Larry's mind-set our relationship can be more meaningful than a friends-only affair, that—

The rec-room phone rings and Reid picks it up, says hello, and listens.

"Eight P.M. Friday? KC's? Sure thing, Dina. I'll be there."

He replaces the receiver. "That was Dina. She's getting the gang together at KC's after the game Friday. She wanted to make sure I'd be there."

Terrific, I think, not looking at him but staring into the crackling fire, watching the charred log crack and split in the angry heat of the flames. Just terrific, I think wearily. So Reid and Dina are still an item.

"Kara," he says, easing down onto the raised hearth.

"Yes?" I ask, glancing up at him.

"I was wondering...about KC's. It's just a casual get-together and—well, would you be interested in going with me?"

Underneath my red wool sweater my heart lurches wildly. I'd love to go anywhere with you, Reid...except KC's. That's Dina's turf and I want no part of it.

"I don't think so, Reid," I say softly. "I—I'm sorry."

Reid turns his attention to the fire. Taking the poker off the rack, he opens the fireplace screen and jabs at the burning log.

"It's okay, Kara," Reid says finally. "I think I understand."

Chapter Seven

"Of course it's a ghost," Tavy is saying. "What else could it be?"

As she speaks, steam from her hot cider rises from the cup in a twisting curve and vanishes between the low-hanging branches of a sycamore.

It's Saturday morning and Tavy, Keith, Carl, Reid, and myself form a loose circle of five, sitting perched on a cluster of the fallen tree trunks that lattice the wood behind Penham's Cider Mill. The pizza article is now history and for the next write-up in our consumer series we're doing a run-down of typical fall activities in and around Lakeview.

Weather-wise it isn't exactly an ideal day to visit Penham's. Most fall weekends the mill does gang-buster's business, but today, with the sun obscured by masses of pearl-gray clouds and the threat of rain hanging in the air like a premonition, business is slow.

Although it's midmorning, the sky has the look of dusk and even the flame-colored maple and oak leaves are dulled by the muted light. Perhaps it's only natural in this gloomy atmosphere that our conversation should have turned from cider and doughnuts to things that stroll through the evening and go bump in the night.

"You haven't got any evidence," Carl mumbles cheerily over a mouthful of doughnut.

"What about the photos?" Tavy asks.

"Too vague," Carl says. "It's just an odd shape. It could be a man, but it's vague."

"Okay," Tavy says. "Say we discount the photographs as evidence. What about Kara's eyewitness account of her encounters?"

"Look," Carl says, "no offense, Kar, but you *have* been known to daydream now and again. I mean, isn't it possible that you imagined all this stuff?"

"Kara is not imagining things, Carl," Tavy replies for me. "My Uncle Brady stayed overnight in the cottage at Strand House about ten years ago. It was part of his fraternity initiation. He says he'd never go near the place again."

"Deciding you don't like a place is not the same as saying it's haunted," Carl says. "Did he say it was haunted?"

Tavy flushes. "Uncle Brady isn't the kind to go into details," she says. "But my Aunt Lauren told me what happened."

"Yeah?" Carl asks. "Like what?"

"Funny stuff," Tavy says. She pauses and takes a sip of her cider. "When Aunt Lauren told me the story she made me promise not to tell anyone. Uncle Brady was starting off his career as an attorney and he didn't want anyone to think he was a kook."

"Go on," Carl urges, one eyebrow skeptically raised.

"Well," she continues, "he's established now and, besides, he moved his practice to California a couple of years back so I don't suppose that it will matter if I tell anyone about it at this point."

"So why don't you tell us?" Carl demands impatiently.

"He told Aunt Lauren he didn't see anything—"

"Aha!" Carl pronounces triumphantly.

"For the first few hours," Tavy finishes with a pointed look at Carl. Hardly chastened he reaches nonchalantly into the wax paper bag for another doughnut.

"Go on, Tavy," Keith prompts, sipping at his cider. "This is getting kind of interesting."

"Well," Tavy says, "Aunt Lauren told me that he heard noises."

"Noises?" Carl echoes.

Tavy nods her head.

"Aunt Lauren says it started with soft rappings on the walls—and then," Tavy says, pausing dramatically, "Uncle Brady saw him."

"Yeah?" Carl says, and for the first time he seems more interested in Tavy's narrative than in the doughnuts.

"He was standing at the window," Tavy says, "gazing out at the lake."

"And?" Carl prompts.

"*And?*" Tavy repeats incredulously. "Isn't that enough?" She throws an exasperated glance in his direction. "Were you expecting gory details or something?"

"Are you kidding," Carl replies, "I live for gory details."

"Well…" Tavy says.

"Yes?" Carl prods.

Tavy swallows and looks out into the woods. "According to Aunt Lauren, the figure in the window turned around and gave Brady a cold, menacing stare and—and Uncle Brady said he knew, without a word being spoken—that he simply had this *feeling* that the ghost was telling him that he was...unwelcome." As she finishes her speech Tavy's shoulders draw up in a small, only slightly theatrical shudder. Carl looks as though he's about to come up with a smart remark, but if he is he's cut short by a sudden misting drizzle that carries the threat of a downpour.

"Uh-oh," Keith says. "So much for tales from the crypt. We've got to tool on out of here right now. That sky looks mean."

Keith is right. Since our arrival at the mill the clouds overhead have darkened and now they look like ugly smears of graphite scrawled against the sky. Even as we get up from our log perches the downpour changes character and big drops of rain start pelting down on us.

"Run for it," Tavy shouts, and we do—quick jogs to the parking lot where Keith's van and Reid's blue Camaro are parked. By the time Reid and I ease into the Camaro we are both breathless and half soaked.

"Hey, Kara—" Reid laughs as he turns toward me "—you look good wet."

"Oh, sure, Reid," I say, as I use the back of my hand to wipe droplets of rain from my forehead and cheeks. "I guess a good dousing of rain beats makeup anyday."

There is a crackle of gravel as Keith's van moves out onto the highway.

"Kara," Reid says, "look at me." His deep voice is touched with an edge of roughness. I glance up into his eyes and for a moment both of us are silent.

He doesn't say anything—but in a way he does. His fingers travel up to my face and trace a delicate path against my cheek, and as I gaze into his eyes I can see that in the dim light they are murky blue, the color of sky before a storm.

It is a magic moment, but, like all my magic moments with Reid, it doesn't seem to have staying power. It dies with a crunch of gravel outside the Camaro. A red Corvette pulls up alongside our car. Through the sheeting rain I recognize Larry and Brad. Brad is signing for Reid to roll down his window.

"Hey, Reid-o, how ya been?" Brad yells over the short space between our cars.

"Okay. What's up?"

"Couldn't reach you at your place," Brad says, his voice loud enough to counter the effects of the pelting rain. "Just wanted to let you know Coach changed practice from two to twelve this afternoon."

"Okay. Thanks for letting me know, Brad. By the way," Reid adds, "how'd you know where to find me?"

"Didn't," Brad said. "Dina sent us over here to get some cider and doughnuts. We're having a little get-together at her place after football practice today, remember?''

''Yeah,'' he says, ''I remember.''

Reid rolls up the window and starts the engine. Soon we are on the highway, driving through the rainy morning, the windshield wipers ticking a mechanical, somehow mournful counterpoint to the steady drumbeat of the rain.

The downpour ebbs slowly and by the time we reach Strand House it has died to a misting drizzle. Reid pulls into the drive and kills the Camaro's engine. We climb out of the car.

''Walk with me for a minute?'' he asks, nodding down at the lake which, overcast as it is now, looks grim and repellent, like a sheet of rippled steel.

''Sure,'' I say and we walk slowly down the sloping red brick path that slices across the front lawn and then turns into a balustraded walkway overlooking the distant expanse of Lantern Lake. At one end of the walkway cement steps curve an irregular path down to the boulder-strewn lakeshore. Reid takes the stairway down to the shore.

I follow Reid to the gravelly edge of the lake. We stand there and listen to water slap over shell, pebble, and sand. Glancing up at him I notice the squint of concentration as he peers out over the water.

"There's the cave opening," he says, nodding over to the shadowed rocks a short walk from where we are standing.

I nod. "They say that's where he used to stash the illegal liquor."

"It's just about in your front yard, too. Ever been inside?" Reid asks.

"Sure. When I was little. My family used to picnic on the lake, and Beth and our friends and I would go exploring. It's shallow as caves go. Runs about ten yards into the hill and then stops. It's really more of a cavern than cave.

"I remember once, when I was about six years old, thinking I'd gotten lost in there. For a while after that I didn't want to do any more exploring."

Reid turns to look at me and I can read the sympathy in his eyes.

"I guess that now and again all of us decide to stop exploring," he says.

"All of us?" I ask. "Gosh, Reid, *you* don't strike me as having any weak spots at all."

Reid smiles. "Don't I? I..." He stops, his voice trailing off. Squinting out at the lake, he begins again. "Sometimes it's hard—always being the new kid in school. My dad's got the kind of job that has us on the move every year or two—he's a quality control engineer with Dynatrol International. Do you know how many branches Dynatrol has in the U.S., Kara?

At least thirty. And sometimes I feel as though Dad's worked every one.''

"It must be hard."

"The worst part is losing all the friends you've made on a regular basis," he says. "And then having to start all over someplace else. I guess," he continues softly, "that's why Dina appeals to me so much—do you know what I mean?"

I nod. Of course I do. But that doesn't stop me from dying inside.

Sure I know what Reid means. How Dina provides him with a ready-made crowd, instant belonging. How, I wonder, did I ever expect to compete with a girl who offers a fringe benefit like that?

I know now that Reid likes me—our moments in the car back at the cider mill proved that to me. So does his honesty. But now I realize that the fact that he likes me doesn't make any difference.

"I understand," I tell him, swallowing hard in an effort to control my emotions.

Sure I understand. I understand that if I want Reid to be part of my world in any important sense I have to become part of Dina's world. I'm not so thick that I don't understand that. And I'm not so thick either that I don't realize that that is a price I don't want to pay.

I look up at Reid reluctantly, hoping desperately that what I'm feeling isn't showing on my face. But it's okay. He gives me a quick smile and then turns his attention to the cave again.

"That dock just outside the cave—that's where they found the second boat," he says.

"Second boat?"

Reid nods.

"I've been reading up on Strand's disappearance, Kara. I went to the Lakeview library and looked through old copies of the *Herald*. According to the stories printed at the time there were two of his boats found shortly after Strand disappeared. One was floating in the middle of the lake and one was still tied to the dock.

"The curious thing is that there were suitcases in both boats packed with identical gear—shirts, underclothing, shaving items: the sort of thing you'd take along on a short journey or a weekend trip.

"The police investigating speculated that Strand was on his way across the lake to the railway station on the other shore. In those days, remember, Lakeview was still an undeveloped wilderness. Even the old two-lane road leading to Strand House wasn't constructed, I've been told, until the thirties. He probably intended to take a train to Chicago where his wife and son had moved a few months earlier. He never made it, though."

"And they never found his body," I whisper.

Reid nods. "The police learned that Strand had somehow managed to get on the wrong side of the mob, and they concluded that the mob was responsible for his disappearance."

He pauses. "There was something else that was odd."

"Yes?"

"Well, when they investigated Strand House the police found no signs of forced entry to the mansion. Whatever happened on the night of Strand's disappearance happened at the housekeeper's cottage. The physical evidence indicated that it had been broken into and ransacked—as though whoever was searching for Strand thought that whatever he had that they wanted could be found in the cottage."

Reid looks out over the rolling waters of the lake, his expression grave. "And there's something else."

"What?"

"Maybe this is a small point, but for some reason it sticks in my mind."

I glance up at Reid expectantly.

"Well, it's what Tavy said about her uncle's experience in the cottage."

"Go on."

"It just doesn't jibe with what I've learned about Jack Strand, Kara. You see, he might have been operating on the wrong side of the law—at least during Prohibition—but everything I've read about him seems to point to the fact that he was—well, a nice guy. The people around here liked him. And that," Reid says, frowning, "just doesn't jibe."

"What do you mean, Reid? Doesn't jibe with what?"

"Well, with the sort of experience Tavy's uncle had. After all, he said that the ghost was menacing—I mean, I'll admit I don't know all there is to know about ghosts—but I do know a little bit about human personalities and—"

"And?"

"And people don't change that drastically— I mean, from good guy to menacing figure."

"Are you sure, Reid? I mean, isn't it possible that, uh, death might affect some people that way?"

I know it's a dumb comment and I want to bite my lip once I say it out loud and hear how it sounds. Sure enough, Reid's deep-throated chuckle signals his amusement. Laughing he draws me to him in a one-armed hug.

"Kara, you're adorable," he says.

I groan inwardly. Adorable? Yuch. That was barely one step removed from cute. Never mind, I tell myself. I'll be more careful about making comments that aren't too well thought out from now on. And as for what Reid thinks of me, I don't really care, do I? With things the way they are we still can never be more than just friends, right?

He's just a friend, I tell myself again, a friend who is practicing his investigative reporting techniques by helping me take an objective look at the goings-on at Strand House. And the fact that he gives great hugs, even with one arm, isn't going to make me forget all that.

"Look, Kara," he says, glancing at the digital watch on his free hand, "I've gotta get going if I don't want to miss football practice, but I think we should get together again and discuss this some more. What we need to do, I think, is gather all the facts we can and then sit down and analyze them logically. At the moment, we don't seem to have any answers. Just questions."

Tell me about it, I think, as I gaze out over the restless waters of the lake which, at the moment, seem to reflect exactly how I feel.

Chapter Eight

Four o'clock. Tuesday afternoon. I am on my way out the heavy oak doors of Strand House, my skates slung over my shoulder, when I hear the phone ring.

I jog down the stairwell to the kitchen, which is where I prefer to use the phone. Mom has decorated the kitchen country-style in yellow and cinnamon, and it's warm and inviting. As I take the receiver off the hook I note that Mom isn't home by the usual clue: the automatic coffeemaker's pilot light is off.

"Kara?" the voice on the other end of the line says.

"Hi, Reid. I was just on my way out the door."

"You don't work at the center tonight, do you?"

"Not Tuesday, no. Actually I was just about to go skating."

"You're really into skating, aren't you?"

"I'm not very good at it."

There is a long pause on the other end of the line. Finally Reid speaks.

"Kara," he says, "why are you so hard on yourself?"

"What?" I ask, startled.

"I mean," he says, "the last time I saw you on the ice you were just letting go and enjoying yourself. And you know something? You were terrific."

"Oh, come on, Reid."

"Look, Kar, I'm not talking about Olympic gold medals here. You...well, I guess it's hard to explain."

"No, I think I know what you mean, Reid," I say softly. "I guess I do tend to be self-critical. Pretty bad flaw, huh?"

"Pretty bad," Reid agrees, his voice wry. "But I guess I'll just have to put up with it somehow. You have to take a friend the way you find her."

A friend. A friend? The word nettles. But why? What do I expect? After all, I'd made a point of telling Reid I didn't think of him as anything but a friend. And I'd made a point of telling myself the same thing, hadn't I?

"What's wrong?" Reid is asking and I realize that it has been my turn to let a lengthy silence hang between us.

"What? Oh, I mean—I'm okay."

"Good. Then instead of continuing this conversation on the phone why don't I grab my skates and join you at the arena? We can talk there."

"Sure, Reid," I answer. "I'll meet you there." There is a click on the line and I slowly replace the receiver on its hook.

The idea of an impromptu skating date with Reid leaves a bittersweet taste in my mouth.

Friends. That is all we would ever be, isn't it? Even if Reid wasn't dating Dina. Even if he wasn't part of her crowd.

And he *was* still part of Dina's crowd, even if he didn't seem to share their values. Try as I might I couldn't overlook that fact.

Alone in the sunny bright kitchen I throw back my head and wrap my arms around myself, fighting back the tears that are stinging my eyelids. Is my life always going to be this way? Like a jigsaw puzzle in which the pieces never quite seem to fit?

The rink is almost deserted. A scant handful of skaters share the ice with Reid and me.

I glance over at Reid. The warm electric lighting brings out the ruddy coloring in his cheeks. He's wearing a cream-colored sweater and jeans and his Bauers move over the ice with a smooth, easy rhythm. Looking up at me, he catches my eye, and smiles.

"You really are something on ice," he says.

"Look, I told you, I'm not anywhere near competition caliber."

"It's not that, Kara. It doesn't have anything to do with standards for performance. I think it's just the way you love the ice. I guess it's just nice to watch a free spirit in action."

"Free spirit? Me?"

"Sure," he says. "Whatever else you may be, you're a girl who thinks for herself."

"Self-critical but independent as the dickens, right?"

Reid laughs. "I have a feeling that the independent side is the real you, Kara."

"I'm sounding more like a split personality by the minute. Thanks a lot."

Reid laughs again, but after we've skated along for a while his face grows serious. I guess I'm being more quiet than I mean to be.

"What's the matter, Kara?"

"Hmm? Oh, nothing...I guess. Except..."

"Yes?"

"Well, I don't know. I guess I'm just sort of wondering whether it's possible that all the stuff that's happening at Strand House—whether it isn't just all my imagination working overtime."

"Oh, c'mon, Kara."

"No. Really. I mean it. Look, I guess you don't really know me all that well, Reid. After all, we only met a couple of weeks ago, so let me fill you in on something. What Carl said that day at the cider mill is true. I mean, I *do* have a reputation for having a wild imagination. I think that's one of the reasons the kids at the center like me. After all, I can sit down with them and spin out a long story to entertain them—making it up as I go along. What worries me is—"

"Yes?"

"Well, I just wonder if I haven't let all the stories I've heard about Strand House affect me."

"Kara," Reid says quietly, "when are you going to start believing in yourself?"

The silence that follows his words is deafening. For a moment angry feelings surge through me and I'm almost ready to tell him where to get off. But I look up into his eyes and I can see that his concern is genuine. I look away.

"You're right, Reid," I say. "I guess it's just that it would be easier to pretend it's all my imagination."

"Easier for how long?"

"What do you mean?"

"Well, since you moved into Strand House, you've seen the ghost three times—each time the moon was full. The pictures I took were taken at the August full moon. Kara, the October full moon is only a few weeks away and I don't see any reason why—"

"Why he should break the pattern?"

Reid nods. "Kiddo, I think it's a safe bet to assume he's coming back with the next full moon."

"That means," I say, "that two weeks from now, Saturday night—"

"He'll be back at Strand House," Reid finishes.

Obeying some unconscious impulse I wrap my arms around myself.

"I could always go spend the night at Tavy's house," I say.

He nods.

"Once a month for the next how many years?" I sigh. "Look, Reid, you're the one who's telling me to believe in myself, aren't you? Well, right or wrong my instincts are telling me that there's a reason Jack Strand keeps coming back to his old house, that there's something that needs to be...resolved."

"If you really want to resolve this," Reid says, "then when he comes back I think you should be waiting for him in the cottage, not in your room."

"Not in my room? But that's where he's always appeared to me," I protest. "As a matter of fact, I thought because I got the east bedroom for my own, I was the lucky recipient of those monthly visits. You do know that Jack Strand used to use my room as a bedroom, too, don't you?"

Reid nods. "I know. But I don't agree with your theory about why he appears to you. According to all the lore I've read, ghosts always haunt—"

"The places that were familiar to them on earth," I interrupt.

"No," Reid says, "it's most often the place where they had some traumatic experience. Usually that translates to the place where they met their ends."

"Oh, Reid, you don't think he died in Strand House, do you? Not in my room?"

"That's just the point, Kara. I don't think he did. If he *was* murdered it was probably in the cottage. As a matter of fact, most of the people who've seen the ghost have seen him in the cottage. Remember Tavy's uncle? And my pictures?"

"But then why—"

"Have you seen Strand in the east bedroom?" he finishes. "I can only theorize, but my guess is that you may be a little psychic. Just as some people are more sensitive than others physically—you may be more sensitive than others psychically. You just happen to be able to pick up on signals and cues that the rest of us tune out. Or—"

"Yes?"

"Or else Strand, for some reason, urgently wants to get some sort of message across to us at this particular point in time."

"So I'm just one of those strange psychic people that pick up on urgent messages from beyond," I say wryly. "But, Reid," I add, sobering, "what *is* the message?"

"That we won't learn from anyone except—"

"Strand."

Reid nods.

"We?" I ask.

"I'm going to be with you," Reid says. Then, grinning, he adds, "Let's consider it a date."

"It won't exactly be a fun date," I say, "waiting for a ghost in a ramshackle old cottage."

Reid doesn't answer, but his gloved hand closes over mine and we skate together, slowly and thoughtfully, over the ice.

Chapter Nine

I don't have any trouble getting a key to the cottage. Mrs. Curran, our housekeeper, lets me have one after I tell her I plan to use the cottage to prepare a surprise for Mom and Zack. That's not exactly a lie, I think, since if Reid and I manage to get to the bottom of whatever it is that's going on at Strand House, I'm sure I *will* have a surprising story to tell.

For a little while I debated telling Mom about the plans Reid and I made for the night of the October full moon, but I finally decided against it. I know from past experience that Mom will attribute whatever I claimed I'd seen to my overactive imagination. And that more likely than not she'd try to talk me out of our nocturnal vigil. And I couldn't take a chance on that happening. Not when we were this close to solving the mystery.

It's a relief to find out that Mom and Zack have chosen the night of the October full moon to take in dinner and a movie. That means I won't have to think up some oddball excuse to visit the cottage.

Outside my bedroom window the twilight sky is gray, tinged at the horizon with coral.

Strand House feels empty, vacated, with Zack and Mom gone. I feel grateful for the noise Mrs. Curran makes as she vacuums the second-floor bedrooms. Sitting at my desk in the east bedroom I can't help but wonder if Reid's plan is actually going to bring things to a head. Or if, as seems quite possible at this moment, I'll simply be made to look a fool.

What if Jack Strand doesn't appear tonight? Will Reid begin to think that I *might* simply be a girl with an overactive imagination after all? And who could blame him if he did? A ghost? In this day and age?

And yet, somehow I know that whatever happens Reid won't doubt me. Possibilities. Things that might be. Reid believed in them. And possibilities allowed for the existence of…of what?

Of ghosts? Of shadows of the past that somehow managed to flicker across the screen of the
present to...to what? To frighten? No, I didn't
believe that. Not that I wasn't frightened when
the apparition made its presence felt. I was. But
it wasn't the kind of fear that came from the
feeling that I was in danger. The fear I felt when
the ghost appeared was, I guess, simply the fear
of the unknown, the unfamiliar. I didn't, after
all, make it a habit to share my air space with
people who had lived and died decades before I
was born.

And the fear came only when the apparition
actually manifested itself.

Now, sitting at my desk, thinking, I am not
afraid. Any fear I may feel is overshadowed by
an odd sympathy.

What was it that Reid had said—about ghosts
lingering behind because they had a message to
deliver? If that was true in Jack Strand's case,
then I could really empathize. How many times
had there been things I wanted to say to the people in my life—my mother, Reid, Zack—and I
just hadn't been able to find a way?

Did ghosts get frustrated the way human
beings did? Was that why Jack Strand had appeared unfriendly to Tavy's uncle? I wondered.
Out of the sheer lonely frustration of it all? Or
was there some other reason? Perhaps the others, for some reason, hadn't been the ones he

wanted to receive his message. Was I the one he had chosen? Maybe that was the case. Lucky me.

My eyes travel to the east window of my room again.

It's raining; droplets crash hard against the glass like pellets of gravel. And over the drumming beat of the rain, a 747 whistles its passage through the rumbling storm, its signal lights blinking against the gray sky that spans the cedars.

I don't know why, but the sight of an airplane cutting across the sky always makes me feel detached and dreamy—especially, I remind myself, when that's the exact opposite of the way I should be feeling.

I sigh. Detached and dreamy might be for other people, but it wasn't for me. Tonight there were certain things that needed to be done.

Still, I can't help but take a moment to deplore the way events always take odd twists for me. I'm almost sure that you could take any other fifteen-year-old girl on this planet, and if you got her involved with Reid Tyler the obvious would develop—movies, football games, parties. Regular dates.

But me? Get me involved with Reid and the next thing you know I'm in charge of locating the key to a rundown little cottage where the two of us will spend the better part of an evening waiting, cheerfully enough, for a ghost to come calling.

Still, odd or not, I remind myself it *is* still a date. And I will love seeing Reid—even if it is on the "just friends" basis that the two of us have found to be comfortable ground over the last few weeks. How terrific, I think, that our friendship can take even such oddball situations as ghosthunting in stride.

And then, suddenly, a horrible thought occurs: What if Reid is interested in me *only* because of the ghost? He had, after all, said that he wanted to be an investigative reporter. Was it possible that I was little more to him than an opportunity to investigate a unique and interesting story?

Outside a distant rumble of thunder rolls across the sky.

A moment later the door to my room creaks open and Mrs. Curran's cheerful round face pops in and announces her imminent departure.

"I'm almost finished, Kara. After I've dusted the downstairs room I'll be off."

"Okay, Mrs. C," I reply.

She turns to go and then pauses.

"Oh, by the way, hon, did you go for a stroll earlier today?"

"No, Mrs. C, why do you ask?"

"Oh, it must have been your stepfather or your mom then—although I'd swear that when

I came in this afternoon, before the two of them took off, that the foyer floor was dry. I have to tell you, Kara, after raising five feisty kids of my own, mopping up footprints has become one of my least favorite cleanup jobs.''

Mrs. Curran registers her complaint good-naturedly enough. I'm sure that as she turns to descend the staircase she's quite unaware of the goose bumps that are rippling my skin.

About half an hour later I'm down in the kitchen putting a kettle of water on to boil, when the doorbell rings. I run upstairs to answer it.

"Hi," Reid says, standing on the front-porch landing. In the moonlight his dark hair sparkles with raindrops. "For some reason I didn't think it was going to rain on the big night," he says.

"Well, you have to admit that it sets the mood for the task at hand," I reply grimly.

"No argument," he answers with a chuckle. "In fact, if Jack Strand was going Hollywood he couldn't have ordered up better weather to make his grand entrance."

"Come on in, Reid. I've just put some water on to boil. I was planning to make hot chocolate for both of us."

"Sounds good," Reid says, stepping into the foyer. Spattered with raindrops he glistens in the light of the chandelier, a tall figure in a cream wool sweater, madras shirt, and chinos.

"Kara, what's the matter?"

"Hmm? What?"

"For a second there it was as though you were looking at me, but you really didn't see me."

"Oh," I say, shaking my head to clear it. "I'm sorry, Reid. It's just that, for a second there, I—"

"What? Tell me."

"Oh, it's silly. It's just that I was thinking about how I felt with you around."

"Oh?" Reid asks, his voice soft. "And how do you feel?"

I look away, feeling funny about telling him, but feeling, too, that he'll understand.

"Unafraid," I whisper.

I don't want to look at his face because I'm afraid he'll be laughing. Instead I continue to stare steadily at the foyer's marble floor.

Reid's knuckles, when they graze my cheek, are gentle. His fingers are gentle, too, as they trace an arc around the curve of my cheek and come to rest under my chin. Tenderly he tilts my chin upward until my gaze meets his.

"I'm glad, Kara," he whispers.

Just then the kettle in the kitchen starts to wail. Reid smiles, dropping his hand from my chin.

"Guess it's time for that hot chocolate," I say, smiling back into his eyes, repressing a sigh.

Reid nods. I turn and lead the way downstairs, Reid following me. As I navigate the staircase, confusing thoughts swirl through my mind.

Reid's touch. His words. They were so tender. Caring. How could a guy who could show that kind of sensitivity feel that it was so important to be one of the crowd, especially Dina's crowd? Oh, Reid, I think as a rush of anger sweeps over me, can't *you* be enough of a free spirit to cut loose from that airhead bunch?

We reach the kitchen and I busy myself making the hot chocolate. My back to Reid, I find myself biting my lip to repress the tears I feel stinging my eyes, tears of anger and confusion. Hadn't I settled, in my own mind, what my attitude toward Reid would be? He would be a friend, nothing else, wouldn't he? Wasn't that what I had decided? And yet how close I'd come to forgetting my resolve only a few moments ago, when Reid's fingers had touched my cheek.

Kara, get a grip on your emotions, I command myself. Concentrate on the tasks at hand, which include serving hot chocolate to Reid and deciding on a plan of action as far as the cottage is concerned.

I pour the boiling water over the powder, stir, then carry the two steaming mugs over to the kitchen table. We sip the frothy concoctions quietly for a while, both of us seemingly lost in our thoughts, the silence between us the only clue to our foreboding.

Halfway through my cocoa I glance up at the kitchen digital clock. 9:05. Reid follows the direction of my gaze.

"I guess you're thinking what I'm thinking," he says.

"That we'd better get over to the cottage?"

Reid nods.

"Do you have the key?"

Reaching into my jeans pocket I pull out the sliver of silver metal and set it on the table between us.

Lightning crackles across the sky as we make the trek past the rain-washed cedars and birches to our destination in the woods. It is, at worst, a three-minute walk from Strand House to the cottage, but the rain is torrential. If it weren't for the umbrellas I've extracted from the brass stand in the foyer, Reid and I would be sodden by the time we reach the door to the little house.

Both of us are carrying flashlights. I shine mine on the door so that Reid can locate the lock and turn the key in it. As we enter the darkened cottage thunder rumbles over Lantern Lake.

Quickly we shut the door. The storm outside becomes muted.

"No electricity?" Reid asks.

"No," I answer, whispering without quite knowing why. "The lines to the cottage were destroyed during a storm years ago, and Zack didn't opt to have them repaired."

"Which leaves us with our flashlights as the only source of light," Reid concludes. "I'm glad I thought to bring one, too."

As he speaks he runs his light over the interior of the cottage. We are standing in a tiny living room filled with odd shapes humped under white canvas tarps.

"What is all this stuff?" Reid asks, pointing to the lumpy shapes with the beam of light.

"Summer furniture mostly. Why?" I ask, closing the snap on my umbrella. "Do you think the contents of the cottage will give us a clue to the reason behind Strand's appearances?"

"Actually I was just wondering if there wasn't some place we could sit down comfortably to await the arrival of our friend from the great beyond."

"Mundane, Reid, mundane," I accuse, laughing in spite of myself. "How about over there?" I ask, aiming my flashlight at two rounded shapes over in the far corner of the room. "Those should serve the purpose. They're wicker porch chairs."

"Super," Reid says.

He starts toward the chairs and the next thing I hear is a sharp cry of pain as Reid crumples to the ground.

"Reid! What happened? Are you okay?" I ask, hurrying to his side. By the moonlight streaming through the window I can see Reid's face twisted in pain.

"I'm not sure," he says, between clenched teeth. "I tripped over something. I think I did something to my ankle."

Squinting at the floor I see the dark bolt of rolled up carpeting, almost indistinguishable from the shadows, over which Reid fell.

"If it's any comfort to you," I tell Reid, "you fell over a very expensive Chinese rug that my Mom's storing here. It's a Benton family heirloom."

"Terrific, Kar," Reid assures me. "Nice to know that it wasn't just any old run-of-the-mill rug that got me."

Then I hear a sharp intake of breath as he presses his fingers over his ankle.

"I can move it," Reid says. "It doesn't feel broken."

"Can you stand up?" I ask, kneeling down beside him.

Reid starts up but when he puts weight on his hurt ankle he cries out in pain and slumps back to the floor. In the faint light of the moon I can see his lips drawn into a tight, compressed line.

"You're hurt," I say, starting up from the floor. "C'mon, we'll go back to the house and I'll call for help."

Reid's hand on my wrist exerts a firm restraining pressure.

"No, Kara. Forget it. We're going to stay right here."

"But your ankle," I protest.

"I'll live," Reid replies, his tone grimly humorous. "At least I think I will," he adds.

"Are you sure about this?" I ask.

"Kara, we decided we were going to resolve this thing and we can't let a little accident set us back. We—" His voice breaks off. "Kara, *look*. Over there."

"Is it—" I begin.

"I don't know," Reid whispers quickly. "It's like...like white mist in the moonlight. Isn't it?"

Bracing myself I turn around. My heart is hammering hard against my chest wall, like storm waves pounding against the lakeshore.

White mist? But mist is vague and insubstantial. You can see through mist. And the figure I see standing in the cottage doorway bathed in moonlight is hardly vague. It is very definitely the figure of a man. And standing there in the shadows he isn't the shimmering miragelike figure I'd seen in my room in Strand House. This figure is—might have been—a real man, a man dressed in an old-fashioned suit, with a thick moustache, and hair slickly combed back away from his face. Unlike the faint figure I'd seen in my room this man is recognizable. This is Jack

Strand, the Jack Strand of the photographs I have seen in Lakeview history books.

"Kara," Reid whispers urgently. "what do you see?"

"It's...him," I whisper back.

"Strand?"

"Don't you see him? He—he's motioning for me to approach. *Reid, what should I do?*"

"I—don't know, Kara," Reid whispers. "You have to decide."

"But how?"

"Look inside yourself, Kara."

"You mean—trust my instincts? In a situation like *this*? What if my instincts are telling me to make a bolt for the door?" I whisper.

"But they aren't, are they?" Reid replies.

"No," I answer. "You're right. They aren't."

I start to stand up when Reid's hand clasps mine and tightens over my fingers.

"Kara," he says, his voice ragged.

"I'll be all right," I say, disengaging my hand from his. In an almost trancelike state, I make my way around the tarp-covered furniture to where Jack Strand stands, beckoning.

"I'll follow you," I say softly.

No reply. Did I really expect one?

"I'll follow," I murmur again.

Still no reply, but the figure slowly turns and begins to make his way into the cottage kitchen. I follow.

It's darker here than in the living room but I find, oddly enough, that I don't have to use the flashlight I'm clenching in my fist. Because, as I follow him, it seems that Jack Strand somehow gives off a faint light of his own, enough light so that when the cellar door yawns open with a rusty clatter and he begins to descend into its pitch-black depths, I can see the steps of the wooden staircase.

Kara, a part of me is saying, what are you doing? This is insane. Totally and completely insane. Following this unearthly figure into a pitch-black cellar when you ought to run screaming out of this place and yell for help. What are you trying to prove anyway?

But another part of me feels itself in the grip of an unearthly calm. Step after step I follow Jack Strand until, at last, there are no more stairs to descend and beneath my feet I feel level flooring.

"We're in the cellar now, aren't we?" I whisper to the figure, whose back is turned to me. "But why?"

Around the softly glowing figure the velvety blackness of the cellar is unbroken.

I have been down here once before. Shortly after Mom and I moved into Strand House, Zack had given us the grand tour. I remember a large room, empty except for the furnace in the corner. All four walls were lined floor-to-ceiling with wooden shelves, all empty.

I clench the flashlight more tightly in my fist, longing to flick it on, but a sort of numbness restrains me. In the meantime the figure that has led me down here stops its slow progression and begins to turn.

In a moment, I realize frantically, I will be standing face to face with Jack Strand. Now I remember what Tavy had told me about her Uncle Brady's encounter with Strand. Will I, like Brady, see a face twisted in a menacing grimace? I hold my breath as the figure completes its slow revolution.

But the face that meets mine is composed, grave. And there is something so resolute and far-seeing in his eyes that, for a moment, I doubt that it can see me. For an odd moment I feel that, to this figure anyway, *I* may be the ghost, the figure that doesn't really belong. Trembling, I lose my grip on the flashlight and I hear it hit the cellar floor.

I realize, just then, that without the flashlight I am at the mercy of my unearthly friend and I find the prospect unnerving. Trembling I stoop down and begin groping along the cellar floor for the fallen object.

Is it my imagination or does the darkness of the cellar intensify as I rake my fingers over the floor? I can't see. Blinking I glance upward only to realize that I'm alone in the pitch-black darkness. Strand has disappeared. For a moment I feel panicked and disoriented.

"Jack Strand," I whisper, "where *are* you?"

No answer. Or is there? I did hear something, didn't I? No words. No. Not a voice. But something. A quick sharp rap. Like the sound of knuckles making short contact with a wooden board.

There, I'd heard it again.

And again.

And then the inky blackness resounds again and again with the sound of feverish knocking. Momentarily I abandon my search for the flashlight and press my hands over my ears to block the nerve-racking clatter.

"Jack Strand," I whisper into the murky blackness of the cellar, "if you're trying to frighten me..." I don't finish the sentence. As abruptly as they began, the noises cease. I put my hands down on the floor beside me to steady myself, and gasp as the fingers of my right hand touch the familiar cold chrome of the flashlight. Laughing with relief, I grab it and fumble for a moment with the switch. I feel ridiculously grateful when at last I have a beam of light.

Standing up I run the light quickly over the cellar. It is the barren, dusty room I remember—with the furnace in one corner and row upon row of tall, empty shelves that had at one time been used for storage. Jack Strand is nowhere in sight.

Great, I think, unable to restrain the sarcasm. Fine thing, Jack Strand. You lead me down into this dank hole, scare me half out of my wits, and then simply disappear. *Now* what am I supposed to do? I thought ghosts were supposed to have some sort of mission. At least that's what Reid's been telling me. But what's your mission? To harass me? Are you just a practical joker like Brad Hamell and Larry Gelhorn?

"Well, *are* you?" I demand loudly, angry enough for a moment to forget that I'm frightened.

"Am I what?" a soft voice behind me murmurs.

My heart turns a somersault as I whirl around, fully expecting to see Jack Strand's pale face looming beside me.

"Reid," I gasp. "How—"

"I startled you. I'm sorry, Kara. I guess you didn't hear me coming down the stairs during all that knocking."

"No, I didn't."

"My ankle finally stopped buckling every time I tried to put some weight on it," he says. He throws an arm around my shoulder and hugs me to him, and I notice that as he does he has to carefully balance his weight on his good leg. I realize that, whatever he says, it is still painful for him to walk, but I'm grateful that he has chosen to ignore the pain in order to come and help me.

"Hey," Reid says, "you're shaking like a leaf."

"Tell me about it," I reply, struggling to form coherent words even though my teeth are starting to chatter. "Listen, Reid, I'm not exactly what you would call a brave person. I mean, abandoned cottages, dark cellars, ghosts, rapping on the walls—those are the kinds of things I usually don't go out of my way to seek out."

Reid chuckles grimly and folds his other arm around me, pressing me to him. The prickly knit of his wool sweater feels absurdly comforting against my cheek. "You not brave, Kara?" he whispers against my hair. "You're one of the gutsiest girls I know. I guess that's what I've always liked about you."

"Always liked?"

"Sure. I always did like you, Kara. I'm really glad we're friends."

"Oh," I say, my disappointment rising by the second.

Friends. That word again. Friends.

Sure, that's all we could ever be, wasn't it? Because Reid might think I was gutsy, and he might like me, but it was more important to him to be part of a crowd I could never be a part of. Thinking about this I become grateful for the darkness, which is only slightly relieved by the beam from my flashlight, because I know that the tears I feel welling up in my eyes will come spilling out any minute.

Suddenly, desperately, I return Reid's embrace, fighting to restrain my tears, as the flashlight dangles precariously from my fingers.

"Hey, Kara," Reid says, his voice soft against my ear. "What is it?"

"It's nothing," I lie, my voice wavering. "It's just that I—I guess all of this is getting to me."

"Tell me about it," Reid says, his voice teasing. "I've got to be honest, Kara. This is not exactly my idea of a good time either."

I try to laugh, but it comes out like a choked sob.

"Look, Kar, we don't have to hang around here. We could leave right now. You don't have to go through all this."

"No," I say quickly, almost without thinking. "No, we have to stay."

"What for, Kar? We've seen Strand. He's led us down here. And what for? Look," he says, taking the flashlight from my hand and shining it all around. "There's nothing down here. Absolutely nothing."

"You're wrong, Reid."

"What?"

"You're wrong. You have to be. Listen, wasn't it you who said that we have to approach this thing logically?"

"Yes, but—"

"Well, let's do it then, Reid. Let's think about what's happened the way we'd think about it if we were investigative reporters: Let's look at the facts and try to make some sense of them. One thing that seems to be apparent to me is that Strand is limited in his ability to communicate with us."

"Limited?" Reid asks.

"Yes. Tonight, for instance. You didn't see him, did you?"

"I saw a sort of mist."

"Well, Reid, I *saw* him. A man. Dressed in clothes from the twenties. He even resembled the photos I've seen of Strand in the library books."

"But when you saw him in your bedroom, you said he wasn't identifiable."

"That's right. He wasn't. And that ties in with what you surmised: That the cottage is where Strand's presence is strongest. Reid, he must be tied to this place for some reason; he either died here or—"

"Or what?"

"I don't know," I sigh. "That's just it. It seems that Strand's ability to communicate is limited. It's limited by place—or else I would have seen him more clearly when he appeared in Strand House. It's limited by time—he can only appear during a full moon. And it's limited by the people who see him."

"I don't get that last point. What do you mean—limited by the people who see him?"

"Just that. You and I were in the same room with him and yet you only saw a mist while I saw the image of a man."

"Which means, I suppose," Reid says, "that you're a touch more psychic than I am."

I nod. "But not by much, I'm afraid. You see, I just realized something."

"Yes?"

"Well, the thing is, I've never heard Strand speak. Apparently I'm not psychically high-powered enough, if you want to put it that way, to receive auditory impressions from Strand. Remember what I told you about his last visit to my room?"

Reid nods.

"Do you remember the circumstances? I was sitting at my window and he frightened me by pointing at me."

"Right."

"It didn't sink in at the time, Reid. But now I'm beginning to realize what it means. It's the only thing that makes any sense of today's sequence of events."

"Go on."

"Well, apparently, since Strand can't communicate verbally, he communicates by gestures. For example, back at Strand House, he wasn't pointing at me. He was pointing past me—at the cottage. Which is where he wanted me to go."

"That makes sense, Kar," Reid says. "But what about tonight? Those knocking sounds I heard. That wasn't you, was it?"

"No," I admit. "It was Strand. That's just it, Reid. He wants us to go somewhere but he can only lead us as far as the cellar. He can't tell us the next step, so he communicates it by a gesture."

"But knocking? What is there down here to knock on? Only these shelves. Why would you knock on empty shelves?"

"I don't know," I say softly, "but I think we can find out."

"How?"

"I think he wants us to take a closer look at those shelves."

Reid turns the beam of the flashlight onto the dusty rows of shelving. I walk over to them and gingerly rap at a wooden backboard.

"That's funny," I say.

"What is?"

"The sound I heard Strand make was hollower, almost as though—"

Reid and I look at each other, riveted.

"We're thinking the same thing, aren't we?" he says.

I nod and move back to the shelves. The two of us start testing the wooden backboards in a rapid, no-nonsense manner.

Only a few minutes later Reid is poised at the section of shelving on the cellar's north wall.

"Kara. Here. Listen to this."

I hear it. A hollow reverberation, a signal that the sound waves are not being absorbed by cinder blocks behind the wood.

"Help me, Reid," I say, taking hold of a section of the shelving.

Reid sets his flashlight down on the floor and together we pull at the shelving. At first nothing happens. But then, with a little more effort, the entire heavy section of shelving starts to move away from the wall. When it is about two feet distant from the wall behind it, Reid retrieves his flashlight and turns to me.

"Ready to look?" he asks gravely.

I nod.

Together we walk behind the shelving. Then we see it: a black irregular opening.

The entrance to a tunnel.

Chapter Ten

Let's go," Reid says, ducking into the tunnel.

I swallow hard and then follow after him.

"Incredible," Reid murmurs as he guides his flashlight beam over the walls of the tunnel. The tunnel is an irregular channel of rock, roughly four feet wide and six high, just high enough so that we don't have to hunch over as we make our way farther into the murky, unfamiliar reaches of Strand's hideaway.

"Look. Over there," I whisper, pointing at the gaping darkness perhaps ten yards distant.

"It's a branch into a wider passageway," Reid says as we approach the beckoning aperture. Then he turns toward me. "Have you ever been in this stretch of cave? I mean back in the days when you were exploring the cave on the lake-shore with your friends?''

I shake my head no. ''Believe me, Reid, I know this area as well as anyone, and as far as I know nobody ever suspected that there was more to the lake's cave system than that ten-yard stretch of cavern under the hill.''

''I'm not too surprised. In fact, it's becoming pretty obvious that Jack Strand somehow discovered this section of the cave and then kept it his own secret. C'mon, let's take a look.''

Reid stoops to pass through the new opening and into the farther reaches of the mysterious underground world that our investigation has uncovered.

Slipping through the same opening, I join Reid on the other side where the walls expand into more generous proportions. All around us my flashlight is picking out the eerie formations of stalactites and stalagmites. And there is something else.

''Listen,'' I whisper.

''Yeah, I hear it, too,'' he says. ''Water. I wouldn't make any loud noises either,'' he warns, aiming the flashlight beam overhead. ''See those ceiling formations? Those things are not exactly powder puffs. They might stay up there for another hundred years or they might fall with the next loud noise. Look, there's one that's crashed into the stream.''

"What stream?''

"There,'' he says, aiming his light a little to the right. "It's an underground system. That's the water we're hearing. Why don't we follow it?''

I nod.

"Let's go,'' he says.

We proceed slowly, partly because Reid still has to favor his ankle, and partly because the world we have uncovered is so strange, simply not the sort of place that you rush blindly through.

"We've walked about fifty yards, Reid,'' I say finally. "And it all looks the same—stretch after stretch of cave. What exactly are we looking for?''

"Shhh,'' he says. "Listen.''

I do as he says and then I hear it. It's like the voice of an old friend, the sound of the lake pounding rhythmically against the shore.

"There it is,'' Reid says. "The exit to the lake.'' The beam of his flashlight dances onto an irregular black crevice in the rocks that's only large enough for a slender man to slip through. It is about twenty yards distant.

Reid nods thoughtfully. "This *was* Jack Strand's secret escape route. Remember the story about his disappearance? According to the newspaper reports the housekeeper's cottage showed signs of having been violently searched. Strand's gangster buddies must have seen him enter the cottage."

"Do you think he managed to escape into the tunnel and elude them that night?"

Reid shrugs. "We don't have the evidence to draw any conclusions. Let's go take a look at that exit."

We begin walking toward the crevice and the sound of the crashing breakers, when the flashlight I'm casually shining ahead of me catches a glimmer of something in the stream that runs alongside our rock path—something startlingly white against the sandy yellow of the cave rock.

"Oh, no," I gasp, staring incredulously at the white shape lying in the stream bed. Pinned beneath the water by a somewhat circular stone about two feet in diameter lies a skeleton.

"Jack Strand," Reid whispers. And then he flashes his light to the cave ceiling just above the skeleton. "See that," he says, making his light dance over the jagged edges of rock that protrude from the ceiling. "Looks like a freak accident. That chunk of calcite must have sheared off from there and pinned him to the stream bed. You can see where the formation broke off."

"But doesn't that mean he was wading through the stream, Reid? Why would he have done that when there's a dry path he could have taken?''

"I think that answers your question," he says, pointing the light to a dark rectangular shape perched on a narrow ledge a few feet above where Strand's skeleton was lying in the water. "Can you guess what's in there?"

I swallow hard. "Do you think it's..."

He nods.

"It all makes sense now. He'd gotten on the wrong side of the mob. He realized he'd have to leave this area pretty soon. He sent his wife and child ahead of him to Chicago, promising that he'd join them as soon as possible, having every intention of doing so. He proceeded to liquidate his holdings, and for safekeeping he stashed the proceeds in this hideaway.

"The mob must have been tipped off somehow about his plans to 'disappear.' They came after him, probably surprising him—so that he had just enough time to enter the housekeeper's cottage. He managed to get to the cellar and pass through the secret passage to the cave before they could get to him. In fact, if it weren't for a freak accident in the cave his escape plan might well have succeeded."

"Too bad he was so dead-set on using the lake as his means of escape," I murmur.

"He didn't really have a choice, Kara. Remember, back in Strand's day the mansion was surrounded by hundreds of acres of woodland, cut through by a single dirt road. He didn't want to risk taking the road because he was afraid he'd be ambushed. So he decided to cross to the other side of the lake in a dinghy. From there he could make his way to the train station that would take him to Chicago."

"But there were two boats, Reid—"

"Sure," Reid says. "One was the actual getaway boat. It was tied to the dock. Strand was going to use that to get to the other shore. The second boat was the decoy. He'd set it adrift maybe a few hours earlier. That was for the police or the mob to find abandoned. He was hoping, no doubt, that they'd assume he'd had an accident on the lake and get off his trail.

"If it weren't for this bizarre accident underground he might have waited here until he was sure his 'buddies' were gone, and then happily made his way to Chicago. Instead, he jumped across this stream, reached up to recover the briefcase with his money that he'd earlier hidden in the cave on that natural ledge over there, and a rock formation that had been hanging onto the roof of this cave for centuries chose that particular moment in time to crash down."

"Knocking him into the stream and pinning him beneath the water."

Reid nods.

"Poor Jack Strand," I murmur.

Reid shrugs, but I can tell from his eyes that he feels a little sad for Strand just the way that I do.

"Should we take a look at what's in the brief-case?" he asks.

I nod.

He hands me the flashlight. "Keep it aimed on the opposite wall," he says. Carefully he jumps over the narrow stream to the ledge on the opposite side. Reaching up he grasps the case, dislodging a small shower of pebbles in the process. In a moment he's back.

With a fragment of calcite, Reid strikes a few blows at the latch of the briefcase and the lock opens easily enough. I lift the lid and blink. For a moment the briefcase seems to be empty, Reid's light falling on black nothingness. Then we realize that the contents of the case are enclosed in black fabric.

"Oilcloth," he says, reaching in to pull out the contents of the case. "It's waterproof."

He pulls out the cloth-wrapped parcel and drops it to the floor. It makes a muffled metallic sound. Fold after fold, Reid begins to unwrap our find.

I repress a gasp as he pulls back a final fold of fabric and the yellow discs that are hidden within catch light and reflect it back. There are hundreds of them.

"Ten-dollar gold pieces," he says, his voice reflecting wonder. "Hundreds of them, Kara. They're worth a fortune. And look, there's something else in here."

Reid pulls it out from under the coins. A yellowing document.

Lifting the fragile paper to the light, unfolding it, Reid begins to read it, his lips moving silently as he scans the paper. "'Last will and testament,'" he murmurs. "'...and all my earthly goods I leave to my beloved wife Eleanora, and, in the event of her death, to my son by adoption, Zack Morris, and to his heirs and assigns forever.'"

"Zack Morris!" I whisper. "But that's impossible! Zack Morris is my stepfather!"

Chapter Eleven

That's right," Zack sighs. "Jack Strand was my grandfather by adoption. I never made it public knowledge because, well, to tell the truth, when they were alive my parents weren't particularly proud of Jack Strand. When they settled in Lakeview, after they'd met in Chicago, they sort of made it a point not to discuss my dad's connection to Strand. Yeah, my dad was the Zack Morris Strand mentioned in his will.

"Personally I don't have any hang-ups about Strand. In fact, I've always kind of liked him. And this crazy old house that he built. When I was looking for a place a few years back and the realtor showed me the mansion, I even had a funny feeling about it—like I was meant to live here. Now I guess I know why." Zack looks at me meaningfully.

"Anyway," he continues, "the price was right and I put my money down. Haven't regretted it, either."

It's just past midnight and the drawing room at Strand House looks like a scene from the conclusion of an Agatha Christie movie. Mom, Zack, Reid, and I are sitting in the drawing room along with Lieutenant Cooper of the Lakeview Police Department.

The flashing red lights of a police vehicle pass under the drawing room window, and I surmise that the earthly remains of Jack Strand are on their way to the Lakeview P.D.'s lab.

"Well," Lieutenant Cooper says, standing up and flipping his notebook closed. "I'm no lawyer, of course, but it seems pretty clear to me, Mr. Morris, that your legal claim to the money is sound."

Zack exchanges a quick glance with Mom, and I think I see something like relief flash over their faces. Then, in a distracted gesture, Zack runs a hand through his tawny hair, raking it smooth with his fingers.

"This is kind of hard to take in," he says. "I mean, that must have been a fortune that the kids found in that cave."

A half-grin passes over the lieutenant's face. "There's little doubt on that score, Mr. Morris. You're one lucky man all right."

Zack's eyes travel to mine and there's a warmth in his expression that I haven't seen in a long time.

"Lucky?" Zack says. "Well, I'd put it a little differently myself, Lieutenant. I think I simply know how to choose stepdaughters. At least I know that when I picked mine I picked a winner—just like her mom."

"Oh, come on, Zack," I protest, uncomfortable under the warm intensity of his gaze.

"No, I mean it, Kara. You are a great kid. I know it now and I've always known it. It's just that—" His voice breaks, and he pauses for a long moment before he continues.

"It's hard to explain all this, Kara. But you deserve to know. Look, I know I haven't been very laid back these last few months. I guess I must have turned you off pretty badly. The thing is, kiddo, going into this marriage I had every intention of being a terrific stepfather. Then last August, things started happening that I just couldn't handle. Well," he says, flushing, "at least not with a whole lot of cool.

"You see, I'm not related to Jack Strand by blood but I do have something in common with the gamblin' old bootlegger. What happened is this: About two years ago, I invested pretty heavily in some high-risk ventures and—well, to make it short, if not so sweet, last August, not two months after your mother and I got married, I found out that I'd lost my shirt.

"Honey, these last three months I've been scramblin' to find a way to hold on to Strand House, keep the wolf from the door, and keep on at my job. I've gotta tell ya, it's been pretty miserable all the way around. I know I probably made it a miserable time for you, too."

"It's all right, Zack," I whisper.

Blinking back my tears I smile at him, the first real and genuine smile I've given Zack in three months.

"Do you think we should have told Lieutenant Cooper about the ghost, Reid?" I ask as I bend over to retie a loose lace on one of my skates.

It's Halloween night, two weeks to the day after our cottage date. Reid has recovered from his sprained ankle and he and I are attending a costume skating party at the arena. Tavy's idea. She wants us to co-write an article on the party for the *Eagle*. I told her I didn't have anything to wear but, as usual, Tavy wasn't taking no for an answer. She got hold of a costume for me, a yellow silk flapper outfit.

"What do *you* think?" Reid asks, as he smooths down the ends of a magnificent, if fake, moustache, reminiscent of an old Clark Gable movie.

He is dressed twenties-style also. He has managed to find a close replica of the style of clothing Jack Strand wore in the history-book photos of him that we've seen. Reid is absolutely the most gorgeous gangster I've ever seen.

"I don't think he would have believed us," I say as I finish tying my lace.

He nods and then lets out a sigh. "I agree," he says. "Maybe it's better to leave it this way: with them thinking we found the cave by discovering the opening behind the boulder on the lakeshore."

"It was an incredible experience, wasn't it, Reid? It's still hard to believe that it all really happened."

"I know," he says. Then he glances over at the ice. "Looks like the Zamboni's finished smoothing the ice. Ready to skate some more?"

"Sure," I say.

I follow Reid back to the ice, which is filling up rapidly with witches, ghosts, devils, and black cats, among other figures. In the center of the rink a lone gorilla is doing a graceful spin.

Reid takes my hand in his and, for what must be the tenth time this evening, I make a mental note to tell Tavy that this is the absolute last time I'll accept a dual assignment with him. It's just too hard, I've decided. These dates that aren't really dates. These feelings that I have for Reid that I can never really express.

"What's the matter, Kara?"

"What?"

"You look a little down," he says.

"I am a little down," I say.

"Yeah. Me, too."

"What?"

"I said, 'me, too,'" he repeats.

"Funny, you don't look all that down to me, Reid." He doesn't either. There's a sort of twinkle in his eyes that counters what he's saying. "Just why should you be feeling bad anyway?"

"Well," he says, "isn't that the way you're supposed to feel when you've lost your best friend?"

"Best friend?" I gasp. "Who are you—"

"Dina," he says, staring straight ahead, with an expression on his face that's just a bit too resolute. "Yeah," he sighs, but his tone is dry as he speaks, "remember when I told you what it was like? Being the new kid in school, I mean? I guess I was pretty darn lucky—moving in next door to Dina and her family. She's been super about making me feel welcome in Lakeview. Kara, that girl is warm-hearted."

Warm-hearted? Dina? Reid had to be putting me on. Didn't he? Warm-hearted. That was a good one.

"Which makes it difficult," he is saying.

"Makes what difficult?" I ask, turning around so that I'm skating backward and facing him.

"Letting Dina down easily," he says.

"What do you mean?"

"I mean how do you tell someone that you appreciate all they've done for you but that you feel it's time to move on?"

Thud! I have landed on the ice in a graceless heap.

"You're moving on?" I say, sitting on the cold, wet arena floor, too startled to get up.

Reid bends down and lifts me to my feet. We have stopped skating and now stand facing each other as dozens of unearthly skaters swirl about us.

"I know why you wouldn't come to KC's with me that time I asked you," he says.

"How—"

"Tavy," he says. "An investigative reporter's delight," he adds, laughing.

"You mean you asked her?"

"I care about you, Kara. I've felt that you cared about me, too. But it seemed that every time I approached you you were turned off. I had two choices: to give up on you or ask questions. And somehow you seemed too important to give up on."

"Oh, come on, Reid."

"If you ever say that again in that tone of voice I'm..."

"Yes?"

"I'm going to..."

"Yes?"

"Do this," he says finally. And he glides toward me over the ice and folds his arms around me.

"Somehow," I say softly, looking up at him, "I don't feel very threatened."

"No?" Reid says. "Good." And he's smiling as his mouth closes over mine. I wonder, as he kisses me, if he feels the same way I do—breathless and slightly dizzy, as if I'm finishing a spin a bit too fast.

After a long moment I pull away.

"That's a pretty stiff penalty," I say softly.

"You bet," he says, smiling, reaching up to trace the curve of my lower lip with a gentle fingertip. "I can be pretty heartless when I have to be."

Looking into Reid's eyes I have the same feeling that I had that day at the ice arena when I caught him looking at me—as if we'd never stop gazing into each other's eyes.

Suddenly the arena doors burst open and a bunch of kids stomp noisily over the rubber matting, yelling greetings across the lobby to each other, looking, I guess, for benches on which to change into their skates. For a moment, I'm afraid that the spell will be broken, but then Reid's fingers close over mine and I'm not afraid of anything anymore.

Take 4
First Love from Silhouette novels
FREE...

and preview future books every month!

That's right. When you take advantage of this special offer, you not only get 4 FREE First Love from Silhouette® novels, you also have the chance to preview 4 brand-new titles—delivered to your door every month—*as soon as they are published!*

First Love from Silhouette offers its readers touching stories about girls...and guys you've known or would like to have as friends. Each novel captures the feelings and thoughts of today's teenagers, and is alive with the kind of characters and situations you can relate to.

As a member of the First Love from Silhouette Book Club, you can get these exciting books delivered right to your door. You'll always be among the first to get them, and when you take advantage of this special offer, you'll be sure of never missing a single title!

As an added bonus, you'll also get the First Love from Silhouette Newsletter FREE with every shipment. Each issue is filled with news about future books and interviews with your favorite authors.

You also get a FREE 15-day examination period on all the books you receive. When you decide to keep them, you pay just $1.95 each, *with no shipping, handling, or additional charges of any kind!*

The first 4 books are yours to keep, and you can cancel at any time. To get your 4 FREE books, fill out and return the coupon today!
This offer not available in Canada.

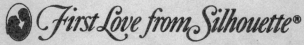 *First Love from Silhouette*®

Silhouette Books, 120 Brighton Rd., P.O. Box 5084, Clifton, NJ 07015-5084

Clip and mail to: Silhouette Books, 120 Brighton Road, P.O. Box 5084, Clifton, NJ 07015-5084

YES. Please send me 4 First Love from Silhouette novels FREE. Unless you hear from me after I receive them, send me four new First Love from Silhouette novels to preview each month as soon as they are published. I understand you will bill me $1.95 each (a total of $7.80) with no shipping, handling, or other charges of any kind. There is no minimum number of books that I must buy, and I can cancel at any time. The first 4 books are mine to keep. **BF28S6**

Name _____ (please print)

Address _____ Apt. #

City _____ State _____ Zip _____

Terms and prices subject to change. Not available in Canada.
FIRST LOVE FROM SILHOUETTE is a service mark and registered trademark.

FL-SUB-2

Delivered right to your door will be heart-felt romance novels by the finest authors in the field, including Diana Palmer, Brittany Young, Rita Rainville, and many others.

You will also get absolutely FREE, a copy of the Silhouette Books Newsletter with every shipment. Each lively issue is filled with news about upcoming books, interviews with your favorite authors, even their favorite recipes.

When you take advantage of this offer, you'll be sure not to miss a single one of the wonderful reading adventures only Silhouette Romance novels can provide.

To get your 4 FREE books, fill out and return the coupon today!

This offer not available in Canada.

Silhouette *Romance*®

Silhouette Books, 120 Brighton Rd., P.O. Box 5084, Clifton, NJ 07015-5084